THE CHEAPEST DATE IN BERLIN

You're never too old to grow up

JOANNA SCHULTZ

Order this book online at www.trafford.com
or email orders@trafford.com

Most Trafford titles are also available at major online book retailers.

Printed in the United States of America.

ISBN: 978-1-4907-2200-9 (sc)
ISBN: 978-1-4907-2199-6 (hc)
ISBN: 978-1-4907-2201-6 (e)

Library of Congress Control Number: 2013923188

Trafford rev. 12/19/2013

www.trafford.com
North America & international
toll-free: 1 888 232 4444 (USA & Canada)
fax: 812 355 4082

Chapter 1

Thirty years is a long time to invest in a relationship that doesn't work. Nora Reinhart had thought about ending hers nearly every year of a fractious marriage. In fact, she dreamed about leaving so often that she had to remind herself that Mitch had left *her* by dying. Consequently, there was no reason to feel guilty, but somehow, she still did.

Why had they married? Nora scrunched her nose up at the question; she was unable to pin down a specific reason for why she married someone who was essentially her polar opposite. Their differences seemed almost endless to Nora. She was blond; he was dark. She was an academic; he was a student of people. Everywhere they went, he found a reason to engage in conversation with strangers—the meaningless chitchat Nora found so annoying. His friendliness and cheery disposition masked a self-absorption that made her feel that she always came in a distant second to himself. This translated into not being able to count on him for much—to be on time, to remember important dates and events, to show her even the basic considerations Nora believed a wife merited.

"Focus on Mitch's positive traits," Nora commanded herself. She would often tell people that he was the funniest person she'd ever met and that was why she stayed with him for three decades.

But did she really believe that? The truth was that in the last half of their years together, he'd stopped being funny. He'd also stopped being attractive. He'd developed that little potbelly so many men past forty acquire. His face grew wider as his hair grew thinner. He favored baggy, unflattering jeans that hid both belly and butt.

Nora kept these observations to herself for the most part. On the rare occasions she'd offered self-improvement advice (thinly disguised criticism, according to Mitch), he'd gotten defensive, looking pointedly at her own expanding middle.

She was still beautiful, though. Her face retained the blush of youth even though she was approaching sixty. She credited her clear, nearly wrinkle-free skin to scrupulous moisturizing. Never go to bed without removing your makeup. Never go to bed angry. Never go to bed before 9:00 p.m. Never go to bed naked.

Lots of "nevers" ruled Nora's existence. Mitch *never* said "never." He believed that absolutes like "never" and "always" limit possibilities. "Keep your options open," he'd frequently said to their sons, Trevor and Michael.

Mitch had opinions on everything. He developed a new crop with every passing year. It seemed to Nora that his mental storehouse, so full of these dictums, ought to have been at capacity long ago. But that didn't seem to be the case. The slim, funny boy she married gave way to the slightly pompous "elder statesman" persona Nora detested.

So really, why *had* she stayed if she felt such disdain for poor Mitch? Was she afraid of being on her own, or did she just think it was better to deal with the monster she knew rather than chance it with something new? Nora wasn't sure of the answer, and truth be told, she was afraid of asking the question. The alternative, she believed, was to become secure in herself. She liked to think she was an intellectual who had the skills and know-how to make it alone under most circumstances, but did she really?

Like so many women of her baby-boom generation, she had sailed from man to man in her youth. As she looked back on her teens and twenties, Nora realized that very little time elapsed between boyfriends. In fact, most every relationship overlapped the one before it. Half of a new couple, the youthful Nora would work up the courage to leave the old one. Nora saw this pattern as suggesting a dependence on men she found embarrassingly outdated.

Nora's female students didn't seem to need men much. Oh, there were a few couples among the many, many singles, but they were the exception. The small college where Nora taught for over twenty years had a lovely chapel where occasional alumni weddings were held, but for the most part, her students seemed reluctant to join forces with someone else when their union might produce a combined student loan debt of $60,000; $70,000; $80,000; or more.

Nora marveled at this practical approach to romance. Her generation had been driven by another force today's students would hopefully never face—the Selective Service. ("Why was it called 'selective' when no one could opt *not* to select to serve?" Nora often wondered.) Nora recalled when she and her first serious boyfriend announced to her parents that they were getting married and moving to Canada to avoid the draft. The war in Vietnam produced many such announcements. Luckily for Nora, the war ended and she and Charlie parted ways before any serious damage was done.

But what should she do with her post-Mitch life? After paying for his funeral, Nora could sail into retirement without much cause for financial worry. On the other hand, she enjoyed teaching. She loved her students. She enjoyed their endearing mix of childlike exuberance tempered by emerging adulthood. But Minton College was over fifty miles from her home in Ann Arbor, Michigan, and the drive was killing her. She'd managed to schedule her classes so she only had to make the trip three times a week. Two of those days, she drove with her old friend Cele who taught history part-time at Minton.

Nora and Cele knew just about everything there was to know about each other. Over the years, they had hashed over their marriages, their classes, and almost everything else except politics. Cele saw herself as a "midline conservative" while Nora retained the self-described "bleeding-heart liberal" status of her youth. In their eight years of commuting to Minton together—through snow, sleet, rain, and the sultry days of late summer—she and Cele managed to sidestep any conversation that might highlight their political differences. Why, then, couldn't she have done the same with Mitch?

Nora and Mitch had fought constantly, but oil and water they were not. Theirs was a more combustible mixture only two people engaged in serial fighting can produce. Things improved a bit after they saw a marriage counselor in the early nineties. At least then, they could see that they were fighting more out of habit than any need to verbally bludgeon each other.

In the first years of their marriage, the fights were nasty free-for-alls of shouting, name-calling, and swearing. One of the worst occurred when her oldest son Michael was six. He was huddled on the couch with chills and a croupy cough. The fight centered on who had the most taxing day ahead and couldn't possibly stay home with a sick child. "I'll go to school, Mommy. I'm OK. Please don't fight," Michael rasped as he struggled to his feet. A chastened Nora stayed home and fumed while Mitch backed out of the driveway with what she saw as a nasty smirk on his face.

Besides their sons, there was one other bright spot in their marriage. They both loved to travel. When the boys were young, they spent a week every summer at a cottage on the Eastern Shore which they rented with Mitch's brother Brett and his wife. They also took several trips to Montana to visit Nora's brother, Cary, who at the time was working as a seasonal park ranger at Glacier National Park. Mitch loved to drive, so most of these trips were taken by car. Nora loathed driving. It was she, not the boys, who would whine, "How far are we? When'll we get there?"

When the boys grew up and left home, Mitch and Nora embarked on their first European trip, ostensibly to join Cary in Germany. Fresh from a painful divorce, Cary decided to try his hand at international teaching and had landed a job at an international school in Berlin. With Trevor in tow, Nora and Mitch viewed great swatches of Germany through the window of their private compartment on one of Germany's sleek Intercity-Express (ICE) trains. Nora smiled when she thought of the lanky expanse of seventeen-year-old Trevor stretched across the dusty seats, dozing through Frankfurt, Munich, Cologne, and Dusseldorf.

What followed that first trip was what Nora thought of as a frenzy of travel outside the US. In their last ten years together, she and Mitch visited twenty different European cities. Although they battled over both the big and little challenges these trips posed, they managed to find common ground in their love of European adventure.

Mitch's approach to travel was freewheeling, preferring to strike out with few solid plans. Nora liked the security of knowing where they'd be sleeping for at least the first few nights of a trip. Over time, Mitch learned to plan a bit more, and Nora's fear of spontaneity diminished. They actually got along much better "on the road" than at home. Even so, their relationship was never ideal.

"I probably could have found someone better for me if I'd waited—been a little less desperate," Nora mused. Then guilt overtook her again. "I shouldn't be thinking this stuff about someone who died." She heard Mitch's voice in her head. "Don't 'diss' the dead!" She giggled at that, in spite of herself. Maybe he still *could* make her laugh.

Chapter 2

Nora waited at the luggage carousel in Tegel Airport, secretly hoping her bags were lost so she could postpone the need to strike out in Berlin. She loved the city, but it had a dark, gritty edge that could easily intimidate. Despite her trepidation, her old red luggage (all five pieces) bounced down the chute and landed at her feet. Grabbing a luggage trolley, she trekked outside to the front entrance of the airport, mentally pulling her shoulders back. She was determined to make a go of this. She had three months to explore every corner of Berlin, even though she knew that much of the time she'd be doing it by herself.

This sabbatical was a last-minute adventure conjured up in late July soon after Mitch's funeral. His funeral had actually been the catalyst. All the sympathetic looks, the hushed expressions of concern, and the question repeated over and over ("what will you do now?") shook Nora out of her torpor. Guilt or no guilt, it really didn't matter. She had to do something with her life, and it might as well include the only dream she and Mitch had shared.

Their "grand plan" was to buy a little flat in Berlin and divide their time between Ann Arbor and Berlin. The timeline was to begin with their retirements—she from Minton, he from Morgan

Stanley. But his cancer treatments took more and more time away from work, and he ended up retiring long before she planned to.

Those last few weeks with Mitch sacked out on the couch when she returned from a day of teaching were the hardest. There was so much they needed to say to each other, but neither knew how to begin. So they both pretended things were as they had always been, with the two of them on opposite sides of every issue. But the Berlin dream persevered, becoming a beacon of hope in their lives. Secretly they each knew that they'd never see Berlin again together, but to admit this was to acknowledge that Mitch was not going to beat the cancer that attacked his colon.

It was Trevor who suggested that Minton might give her a few months off to come to terms with the loss of her husband. She wasn't due for a sabbatical until the next school year, but the college's dean bent the rules to allow her to take a semester off with pay when she needed it most. This uncharacteristically kind gesture by the dean caught Nora off guard. She felt compelled to do something meaningful with this unexpected gift, even though what she really yearned for was to snuggle into her favorite chair with a stack of romance novels. But Trevor persuaded her to take the sabbatical in Berlin as a way of testing the waters of her dream.

Nora knew Trevor had serious reservations about her ability to carve out a life for herself in Europe, even on a part-time basis. She would prove to him that she could fend for herself. Besides, her brother Cary and his new wife, Monika, were firmly entrenched in married life in Berlin. The real challenge was not to become dependent on them. She knew it would be tempting to turn to them when the blues struck—as they inevitably would—but she was determined to stand on her own two feet in the city she considered her second home.

A long line of taxis were parked in front of Nora as she stood at the curb in front of the airport contemplating her next move. Cary was teaching and Monika was out of town, so she had to make her way to their house on her own. To save her precious euros, she knew she should take the X9 bus to a nearby S-Bahn station and take a local train to Lankwitz where Cary and Monika lived. But jet lag was already blurring the edge of consciousness, so she opted for a taxi as the least ambitious (but most expensive) route. Besides, she told herself, she needed to dust off her German. Directing the taxi driver to Lankwitz was a good place to start. She hauled her luggage to the beginning of the line of taxis as previous visits had taught her was SOP in Germany. Rule 2: Always ask what the fare will be before you get into the cab. *Ich brauche nach Lankwitz fahren. Wie viel kostet das?* This was the German way, Monika had taught her. The driver smirked at her accent but agreeably responded, "*Fünfundzwanzig*" (twenty-five euros).

Nora considered everything she could do with twenty-five euros—versus the five euros the bus-train route would cost her—but decided that the opportunity to take the more scenic and less physically demanding route was worth the money.

They glided past the giant rolled-up newspaper sculpture on the road out of Tegel. Nora settled in for a glimpse of the first of her personal landmarks—the Jack Wolfskin store in Steglitz. She knew that if she hopped out at the large outdoor camping store, she only needed to walk four blocks to her favorite destination in Berlin—Hugendubel, the popular German bookstore with branches all over the country. She'd spent many satisfying hours nursing a cappucino at the bar in front of the windows of the second-story Hugendubel cafe in Steglitz, captivated by the people scurrying to and fro on the street below. Each carried a cloth shopping and a look of determination. They would find what they were shopping for or die trying!

But there'd be lots of time for Hugendubel. Meanwhile, she found herself experiencing the same anxiety that always struck her in a foreign taxi. Was the driver going the right way or was he wending his way lazily through the city, eating up time and miles as the meter ticked five . . . seven . . . twelve . . . twenty-five . . . thirty euros? Mitch never worried about the ethics of taxi drivers in Europe, even that time when a taxi driver in Paris raced through the streets at ninety miles an hour to proudly deposit them at Charles de Gaulle long before their flight was due to board. "You are early, madame and monsieur. I drive well, non?" They nearly fell out of the cab; so grateful were they to be alive.

Nora glanced at the seat beside her, half expecting to see Mitch with his nose glued to the window, ready to narrate their progress through Berlin. Nora felt a tiny stab of pain. Mitch would have loved this extended stay. The longest they'd visited the city in the past was three weeks in 2004 when they both attended a German language school in Berlin's Wilmersdorf district.

Nora both delighted and dreaded the thought of the three months that lay ahead. Ostensibly, the goal of any sabbatical was to conduct research. She did plan to do a modest research project on the stories former East and West Germans tell about the aftereffects of the fall of the Berlin Wall. But she didn't consider this really serious research. She had no intention of publishing the results of this project. She was moderately interested in the subject, but not enough to really throw herself into it. She would dabble a bit, just enough to give a convincing report to the dean and the sabbatical committee. What she really wanted to do in Berlin was overcome her fears of being alone. But how to do that other than actually *being* alone?

The taxi meter ticked and stopped at twenty-four euros. She told herself, as she always did, that she was silly to assume that all taxi drivers were bent on ripping off visitors. The driver unloaded her baggage. He even carried it to Cary and Monika's tiny front porch. Nora tipped him generously. He looked disapproving but accepted the money anyway. Nora watched him drive away, already missing this minimal human contact. Cary wouldn't be home for hours, and Monika wasn't due back from her business trip to Frankfurt until the weekend. Only Meister, the cat, was there to greet her when she unlocked the front door with the key Cary had hidden in a flowerpot.

Nora was not terribly fond of animals, but Meister had a benign, inoffensive personality except for his habit of dropping little gifts—dead mice and wingless birds—at her feet during a previous visit when Nora house-sat for Cary and Monika.

The house was just as she remembered it: small from the outside but with a surprising number of rooms inside. Nora entered the foyer with its collection of shoes. Monika requested that everyone take off their shoes at the front door (except Meister, of course, whose midnight "catting" often brought him home with muddy paws and a coat encrusted with burrs).

French doors led from the front hallway to the living room with the raised platform of the breakfast room visible beyond. A skylight in the breakfast room poured sunlight on the table beneath, casting a golden glow over the morning's half-empty teacups. A door opened off the breakfast room that led to the backyard. Oops, Nora forgot—in Germany it was a "garden," not a backyard.

A wave of fatigue swept over her. She headed down to the basement where the guest room was located. She dove gratefully into a fluffy duvet on the bed, promising herself that she would just rest her eyes. Every experienced European traveler knows that one must never nap on the day of arrival. One needed to stay up until the normal bedtime to ease one's body into its new biorhythms.

Ignoring this rule, Nora woke hours later when Cary shook her shoulder gently. "You need to get up," he said. "Dinner's ready, and you're never going to get to sleep tonight if you don't get up now." Good advice, but Nora suspected that she'd already nixed any chances of falling asleep later. She was now full of the adrenaline that fueled the start of the first day of every new trip. She leapt out of bed and splashed cold water on her face. Her first dinner in Germany awaited.

Cary had made one of his specialties—chili with corn bread. Cary was an excellent cook. He'd even cooked briefly at several restaurants in the US Park Service before he began his teaching career. Cary was sixteen years younger than Nora. She still sometimes thought of him as her first child. His unexpected birth brought a new warmth to her family. Before Cary's birth, things had been pretty dark at home with a moody young girl rapidly approaching adolescence. Then Cary was born. His sunny disposition brought Nora and her parents together in their mutual adoration of the tiny blond cherub who suddenly brightened their lives.

As Cary grew, Nora took him everywhere. They often went to the local K-Mart to look at the pet turtles. Cary was desperate for a turtle of his own, but their mother put her foot down. "No more pets! I've got my hands full with you two." And that was that. But Cary could still look longingly at the turtles in their plastic dishes with the tiny plastic palm trees.

Nora lost interest in the turtles long before Cary did. She would often say "I'll meet you at the turtles in ten minutes," assuming Cary would meander over to the toy aisle or to the front of the store with its kiddie carousel. Once, she hid behind a dog food display in the pet department, anxious to see where he'd go after they'd agreed to meet later. She was amazed to find that he never left the turtles. Instead, he reached a small tentative finger into a dish and tried to coax the tiniest of the turtles into his hand.

Forty years later, Nora could still close her eyes and see that little boy who became her best friend. She often thought that a man like Cary—someone more like herself—would have made a better choice for a spouse, although the adult Cary was sometimes a tiny bit crotchety. Monika dismissed this simply as being "grumpy."

Nora had shared many significant experiences with Cary. They'd walked the streets of Paris from one side of the city to the other. They'd traversed the klongs of Bangkok in a longboat. They'd even discovered their grandmother's ancestral home in Charleroi, Belgium, only to find that it had been converted into a Tae Kwon Do studio, any traces of their mother's French relatives long gone.

In their travels around Germany, Nora and Cary often speculated about what motivated the Nazi lust for Jewish blood. They often sought an answer in movies. They viewed *The Pianist* together in the big English-language *Kino*/movie theater in Potsdamer Platz. They marveled at the elegance of Adrian Brody's performance as the Jewish musician in Poland who goes "underground," protected from the wrath of the Nazis by a sequence of friends and admirers. Acquaintances of Cary's—a German wife with her American husband—offered Nora and Cary a ride home from the cinema. The four got into a lively debate over whether present-day Germans should feel guilty over what the Nazis did to the Jews. The husband, perhaps out of a desire to protect his wife from scrutiny by the two bolder Americans, suggested that today's Germans should feel no more guilt over the Holocaust than Americans should feel over slavery. Nora and Cary later agreed that the two situations were simply not at all the same.

Moviegoing in Berlin is a much more formal experience than it is in the United States. For one thing, seats in most theaters must be reserved much in the same way as concert seats. One always arrives thirty minutes before a movie begins to sit through one commercial after another. "Why do they put up with that?" Nora once asked Cary who, by then, seemed to have a good grasp on German behavior. Cary thought for a moment. "Because it's what they do," he said, realizing as he said it that he'd touched on everything and nothing about the German psyche.

"What are your plans now that you're actually here?" Cary asked as he spooned the last of the chili into his bowl.

"I've got the research project I told you about, and I'm also thinking about going back to the Neue Schule for more German classes."

"Are you sure you want to go back there after last time?" Cary asked. Nora considered this. Her first course at the Neue Schule *had* been challenging, mainly because nearly every student in the class was at least twenty-five years younger than her. They were mostly eighteen-, nineteen-, and twenty-year-olds studying for the German proficiency exam they needed to pass before they could study at a German university. Of the twelve students in the class, all but one were under twenty-one years old. The only other "older" student was an ancient thirty-five.

Nora joined a class already in progress. Most of the students started the class as beginners and advanced to Nora's level of proficiency—such as it was—after two months of introductory lessons. Her classmates came from all over the world, and just as Nora had entered the class "midstream," other students came and went. At one point, the class included students from nine different countries.

An initial placement test determined the class in which each student was placed. Nora considered this a beneficial system. It meant she was at just about the same level of proficiency as her new classmates. However, this proved to be only part of the equation.

Nora's classmates reminded her of the students she taught in the US. They all aspired to earn BA or BS degrees. Nora had completed her doctorate years before. To be back in the classroom as a student with classmates who were young enough to be *her* students felt very strange. To be one of the slowest in the class (when it came to German, Nora was a plodder) in a group of sharp young minds who grasped concepts far faster than she was decidedly humbling.

The teacher's name was Anya Mueller. She was a reed-thin runner addicted to cigarettes and worksheets. The first hour and a half of their three-hour class was devoted to grammar drills. In round-robin fashion, each student supplied a missing word in a sentence or chose a correct verb form from several possibilities. Standard classroom stuff for kids, but not for a class of college-age (and above!) students, in Nora's opinion.

Despite her skepticism about Anya's teaching methods, Nora usually supplied the correct answer—but only after a long, long pause to weigh possible alternatives. Her young classmates blasted through these exercises without faltering. After a few weeks, Nora figured out why. Like elementary-school kids, they were counting the number of students between the current student's "performance" and themselves. They then looked up the answer to *their* question in the answer section of the textbook. Naturally, each had the correct answer ready long before it was his or her turn in the spotlight. "Nora the plodder" would try to figure out her answer only when her turn came. She trusted that she could discover the right answer by translating the other words in a phrase or sentence. But unlike Nora, her young classmates were not interested in what the German words in these exercises meant. They only cared about having the right answer when it was their turn at bat.

The low point in the class for Nora came one morning when she had struggled several times after her classmates rapid-fired their answers on the eighth worksheet of the day. Nora studied the missing word in her sentence, determined to get it right. The answer popped in her head, and she blurted it out triumphantly. Unfortunately, it was the answer to the question *before* hers. She was so intent on figuring out her answer ahead of time (yes, she'd learned to do this too) that she miscalculated how many questions came before hers. She hadn't listened to the student ahead of her who had already supplied the correct answer. Her blunder was greeted by a loud guffaw from Jovanna, a female student from New Zealand.

Nora saw red. The god of righteous anger rose up in her. She became the defender of all weak and powerless students who had ever been ridiculed by their classmates. "DON'T LAUGH!" she roared, with a lot more force than necessary. Jovanna, who happened to be a quick study in German, was taken aback. "I wasn't laughing at you," she assured Nora. She was supposedly laughing at a joke Michael from Italy who sat next to her mumbled under his breath. This, Jovanna maintained, had nothing to do with Nora.

But Nora wasn't buying it. She had watched Jovanna direct plenty of ridicule at Sotoru from Japan, the second-worst student in the class, on many occasions. Anya rose to Jovanna's defense, both then and later in the hallway outside the classroom. Nora didn't tell Anya she'd noticed that laughing at others' mistakes seemed to be perfectly acceptable in the class. She had witnessed Anya routinely joining in the laughter. Nora liked Anya and didn't want her to feel bad, but the professor in her believed a good teacher needs to err on the side of students who struggle, not on the side of students for whom learning comes easy.

After this interaction, Nora was careful not to draw undue attention to herself. Anyway, after her confrontation with Jovanna, the atmosphere was usually pleasant. Nora even tried to make up with Jovanna by asking her about books she'd read (Jovanna, too, was an avid reader) and offering to share her limited supply of English-language novels with Jovanna.

Nora thought about this incident often. Why did she feel so guilty about calling out Jovanna for her bad behavior? Had she violated some unspoken rule about students who were different maintaining a low profile in class? Or was she uncomfortable about slipping inappropriately into her professorial persona?

Before her experience at the Neue Schule, Nora had always been a power broker in the classroom. The power she held was of "she who possesses the knowledge and bestows the grades." Nora had no power in her class at the Neue Schule, not even the limited power wielded by the smart kid who always knows the answers. *She* had been that smart kid in her graduate classes. She wasn't used to being slow, and she didn't like it one bit. She wasn't sure how to act under these circumstances, and as when she thought about the incident with Jovanna, she saw her outburst as not at all in keeping with her usual sense of self.

"What's with these kids who think they're something special just because their skin is smooth and their abs are flat?" Nora ruminated. She sensed that the status system at the Neue Schule was heavily weighted in favor of twentysomethings. Their meager life experiences trumped hers simply because they could drink all night and arrive in class the next day with hardly any sign of wear on their beautiful young bodies.

At Minton, the coin of the realm was a university degree. In that world, Nora was a queen, possessing the terminal degree in her field. Her title—Dr. Reinhart—automatically commanded respect and deference. Doors were opened for her. Students stepped aside to let her pass. Even students she didn't know greeted her by name on her campus walkabouts: "Good morning, Dr. Reinhart." No, she was definitely not prepared to be low woman on the academic totem pole.

Nora discovered her intellectual side later in life than most. She'd been a mediocre student in her undergrad days, more interested in what was happening off campus at friends' apartments than in her classrooms. She excelled in the fields she enjoyed— English and theater—but expended little energy on classes in which she had no interest. Consequently, her transcript was filled with A's and D's, averaging an underwhelming C.

After Michael was born, she considered graduate school. When she interviewed at her undergrad university, an admissions officer saw something in Nora and allowed her to enroll in a master's program in theater on a probationary basis. Something changed in Nora since her twenties, and she sailed through her master's and doctoral programs with all A's. She delighted in her new sense of academic prowess. She had always had a pretty face. Now she had a lovely mind to match.

"Do you really want to be in a class with all those young kids again?" asked Cary.

"Nooo . . . I don't. Maybe I'll just look for a conversation partner instead."

"I talked with Gerd the other day. He's looking for something part-time to supplement his pension. Maybe he'd be good."

"Great idea! I'll call him tomorrow and see what he thinks!"

Suddenly, Nora felt another deep wave of fatigue. Jet lag reared its ugly head again. "I think I'll turn in," she said.

"Hope you can sleep." Cary sounded doubtful. After all, she had violated the never-go-to-sleep-on-the-first-day-until-your-regular-bedtime rule. Nora didn't tell Cary, but she fully intended to take a sleeping pill—something she normally reserved for the second night of travel.

"Who's gonna know?" she reasoned. "It's only me now."

Chapter 3

When she woke the next morning feeling surprisingly rested, she thought about Cary's suggestion about asking Gerd to be her conversation partner. "Hmmm," she thought, "I wonder what he's up to these days." The last time she saw Gerd was at protest rally against the invasion of Iraq in 2003. This antiwar demonstration was held in Alexanderplatz in the heart of what had been East Berlin.

Gerd had met her on the train platform in Alexanderplatz. He and Nora left the station and stepped into the surrounding square. They were immediately engulfed in a sea of protesters. Nora wasn't sure what she'd expected the rally to look like, but the sheer volume of the crowd was astonishing. Later on the TV news that evening, she learned that the demonstration in Alexanderplatz had drawn over ten thousand protesters.

An army of policemen directed the flow of bodies out of the square and into a nearby street. Nora saw a sign that read "Karl Marx Allee." Her heart skipped a beat. This street was the scene of many organized protests during the Cold War. Nora felt as if she'd wandered into a forbidden zone where she could easily be corrupted by forces outside the control of the American government. When she saw a straw figure of George Bush burning in effigy, she determined to be as unobtrusive as possible.

But Gerd was having none of that. Whether he was proud of having an American friend or anxious to establish his political distance, he insisted on introducing Nora to many people in the immediate vicinity of the speaker's platform. Nora braced herself with each introduction, fearing a tirade against Americans, but none came.

Quite the opposite. Everyone she spoke with wanted to explain their own unique perspective on the war. There were members of different political parties, gay groups, religious groups, university students, and high school students. Each group put their own spin on the issues.

Nora observed that the German language seemed particularly well-suited for strident speech. The Germans even have a special word for this—*Schreierei*. Although she couldn't understand the words of the main speaker, Eric Stoibel, who later ran unsuccessfully against Angela Merkel for German chancellor, Nora certainly understood his tone. Thank heaven the wrath of the protesters was directed at the American government and not toward the lone middle-aged American woman in the crowd.

Nora had only one reservation about resuming her friendship with Gerd. Although he was a nice man with an old-world courtliness about him, he had confessed to her that he was frustrated with the pension he received as a retired teacher from Berlin public schools. His father, he revealed to Nora, had been a Nazi and an officer in the German army during World War 2, and had received far better benefits than Gerd in the newly unified Germany.

Nora was sure she misunderstood this at the time but later read in the *Detroit Tribune* that the German government had come under fire for admitting to paying convicted Nazi war criminals "supplementary pensions" while many of the Nazis' victims received no compensation. A German Labor Ministry spokesperson confirmed that billions of dollars were being paid each year to thousands of former Nazis who suffered a disability linked to World War 2. This was on top of their normal pensions.

Nora knew it was unfair to judge Gerd for whatever his father might have done—and here her imagination veered off in a thousand directions—but she had a hard time reconciling the picture of pleasant, mild-mannered Gerd with that of a Nazi offspring. "Get over it," she told herself firmly.

Cary was teaching a morning class, but he left his address book on the kitchen table. He knew Nora well enough to know she would follow up on his suggestion right away. Nora was a "do it when you think about it" kind of gal. Mitch had been a "let me think about it a while" kind of guy. This was another point of dispute in the great divide between Nora and Mitch.

"Schneider here," Gerd answered his phone in the traditional German way.

"Gerd? This is Nora Reinhart, Cary Weismer's sister from the US? I don't know if you remember me." Nora's voice shook a bit.

"Ya. Of course I do, Nora. Are you here in Berlin?"

"Yes, I'm on sabbatical again. I'm staying with Cary and Monika until I find a place of my own."

"You should have no trouble. There are many, many flats available in Berlin."

"In the meantime, I am looking for a conversation partner to help me with my German. I can pay ten dollars . . . oops, I mean twelve euros a session. Are you interested in doing this?"

Nora was not sure she had phrased this tactfully. She certainly didn't want to insult Gerd in some way. Might he misinterpret this as a request to pay him for his friendship?

Gerd chuckled. "Did Cary suggest you call me? That would be so like him. I complained to him about my pension. You really don't need to help me with this. Your German is most likely fine."

"Not really, Gerd. It's still not very good. I can speak it all right, but it's so hard for me to respond when someone says something to me in German. I panic and I have to ask the person to repeat whatever they said again. It's like my ears don't work right when I have to use the German side of my brain!"

Gerd laughed again. "I'm sure you are exaggerating, but I'd be happy to meet with you so we can discuss this further. Would you like to come to my flat tomorrow for tea? Perhaps at sixteen hundred?"

Nora smiled at his use of military time. Then she grimaced as she thought briefly about Gerd's father in the German army. "OK. I'll be there." She shook off her misgivings and said resolutely, "Cary knows where you live, so I'll have him draw me a map. See you tomorrow."

"Nein, we must say *bis Morgan* (until tomorrow)."

"Oh yes, *bis Morgan.*"

Gerd sounded just as she remembered him. He spoke the formal British English so common among most of the proficient English speakers she knew in Berlin. Like many people from the former East Germany, Gerd had studied Russian in school. His English was learned at an intensive language school in London where he traveled after his university days in Berlin. He told Nora the last time they met that he relished any opportunity to speak English with a native English speaker. He had taught in German and most of his friends spoke only German, so he had few chances to use the English he was so proud of.

"OK," Nora said to herself. "That's one thing taken care of. Now for an apartment." Cary and Monika had found a tiny vacation flat for Nora (a *Ferienwohnung*) within easy walking distance of their house, but Nora hesitated to look at it. It was too convenient. If she took the flat, would she be more likely to rely on Cary and Monika's house as her real home base in Berlin? Nora reluctantly agreed to look at the flat to please them, but she was already conjuring up an excuse for not taking it.

She called the owner of the property who happened to be cleaning the flat between rentals. Stumbling through their conversation in German, Nora made arrangements to meet with the flat's owner within the hour.

She borrowed Monika's bicycle and headed off for the flat, which proved to be about five American blocks from Cary's. It was actually one of two small short-term rentals in a concrete structure located behind a much larger house where four long-term flats were located. Nora concluded all this from the mailboxes near the front door of the house. There were no mailboxes on the concrete structure. The landlord—actually, land*lady*, to be exact (and goodness knows, Germans are anything but inexact!)—opened the door to the second of the two holiday flats after Nora's timid knock. "Come in," she said in German.

Nora stepped inside and took in the flat's tiny living/dining area with its good-sized bedroom beyond. A teeny-weeny kitchen nestled in one corner of the living room. A small table and two chairs comprised the dining area. There was a generous couch with a well-worn coffee table. A large television on a cart completed the furnishings in the living/dining area. The bedroom featured two single beds and a large wardrobe. A perfectly adequate bathroom (no tub but a standard German shower stall with its standard sticky door) off the other end of the living room completed the flat.

After surveying the flat and its furnishings, Nora noticed something peculiar. Although it was at least eighty degrees outside, it was downright chilly in the flat. She had a fleeting desire for her snuggly black fleece.

She decided that the flat was OK but cold—cold in temperature and cold in atmosphere. The concrete walls and tiled floors did nothing to "cozify" (as Mitch would have said) the space. Could she find a way to bring a little warmth to the flat, or was it a lost cause?

She thanked Mrs. Dietrich, the landlady, and promised to call her the next day with an answer. She was leaning heavily toward "no."

She debated with herself on the way back to Cary's. The flat was cheap enough—only five hundred euros a month—and didn't require any sort of security deposit or cleaning fee. No first and last month's rent either. It *was* close to Cary's, but was it too close? The garden behind the flat was pleasant, a great place to linger with a good book, but would Nora feel comfortable hanging out in this common space? Did she have as much claim to it as the residents of the big house? She planned on buying a bike to use in Berlin, but would it be safe to park outside the flat? A large stucco fence enclosed the property and hid the house and the concrete structure from the street. Would this be enough to protect her bicycle from a determined thief with a chain cutter? She'd read that bicycle theft was the most common crime in Berlin.

Nora weighed the pros and cons of the tiny flat as she boarded the S-Bahn train ("S" for *Schnell*—fast). She had a long ride and two transfers to get to Gerd's apartment on time.

Riding on European trains was one of Nora's favorite pastimes, especially in Berlin, where the transportation network was amazingly efficient. In the many times Nora had ridden Berlin trains, she'd observed the unspoken rules of German train-riding. Near the top of this list of do's and don'ts were the norms for appropriate space occupation. Passengers were expected to occupy the smallest space possible. This meant no crossing legs, no slouching, and absolutely no spreading out across two seats with one's arm casually flung over the back of the adjoining seat (the typical pose of American tourists). Ironically, if you had bags or a backpack, it was OK to place these items on the seat next to yours. It was practical and, therefore, permissible.

Loud talking was seriously frowned on in the trains, unless you were part of a group of rowdy soccer fans returning from a match where lots of beer was consumed and you were wearing a scarf in the home team's colors. Reading a book was de rigueur, but listening to music where others could hear it was not, unless you were among the endless bands of roving musicians who serenaded passengers on the trains and in the stations.

There was generally silence among train passengers. (Trevor once cautioned his talkative father, "Dad, train time is quiet time.") This did not apply to "down and outers" who frequently jumped onto a train car at a station and proceeded to recite sad tales of woe to their captive audiences before circulating among the passengers with an empty paper cup and a humble *klein Geld, bitte* (small change, please).

Perhaps the most important tenet of train-riding was "never smile at anyone," either in the station or on the train. A German friend once confessed to Nora that Germans secretly thought Americans were a little addled because of their habitual (and, Germans assumed, meaningless) habit of smiling for no good reason.

All these rules made train-riding in Berlin an intensely private experience. "Maybe," thought Nora, "that's the point. If you need to move across space and time in an enclosed space with a bunch of strangers, perhaps one pulls on the 'cloak of autonomy' very tightly to maintain a sense of privacy."

Nora saw herself as an experienced train rider, but there was one aspect of riding the trains that still caused her more than a little angst. Whenever a train engineer made an announcement, Nora panicked. Announcements were usually made by the officials in the stations. An engineer's announcement on a moving train was unusual and almost always meant trouble. His or her rapid-fire German, spoken with slurred words and a guttural delivery, was almost impossible for Nora to decipher. She would anxiously scan the faces of her fellow passengers after such an announcement. Were they simply making the German equivalent of the "tsking" sound of mild frustration, or was she hearing a chorus of *Sheise*s (shit!) that signaled a major inconvenience? The worst was when they gathered up their bags and fled the train car. Nora would frantically search for someone who looked like they might speak English to ask "*Was hat passiert?*" (What happened?). People always seemed to be in a hurry then and didn't want to bother with an *Auslander*/foreigner.

Her worst experience with "train trouble" was when she was traveling to the main Berlin train station, the *Hauptbahnhof*, to transfer to another line. The train had only made four stops when it ground to a halt at Westkreuz, one of the larger stops on the S-25 line. An ominous announcement was made by the engineer, and the other passengers bolted for the door. Nora followed. On the platform, at least forty members of the Berlin *Polizei* stood in groups of four and five, some wearing flak jackets, most carrying ugly-looking weapons. Nora had no idea what was going on, but she sensed that she'd best get out of the station as soon as possible. She found an agreeable-looking female officer and asked her how to get to the Hauptbahnhof. Listening carefully to the officer's directions, Nora understood her to say there was a bus stop just outside the station from which she could get a bus that, after several transfers, would eventually get her to the Hauptbahnhof.

The bus arrived just as Nora got to the stop along with many of her fellow passengers from the S-25 train. Settling into her seat, she asked another passenger what had happened at the station. "A bomb threat," a German businessman stated in a hushed tone. Perhaps it was good that she hadn't understood the engineer's announcement. Panic may have kept her from finding the right route. The bomb threat proved to be a false alarm, but the incident further confirmed Nora's belief that she really had to work on her German if she was to meet the everyday challenges of life in Berlin.

Whether it was a need to change trains or a problem with the line that necessitated an alternative form of transportation, Nora was often forced to alter her planned route or wait endlessly on a crowded platform, other passengers tapping their feet impatiently. She felt safe in blessed anonymity only when she was back on a train bound for southeast Berlin. Heart pounding, she would settle into the seat nearest the door, ready to escape when her train pulled into the Lankwitz station.

The inevitable happened again when she set off for Gerd's flat. A garbled announcement followed by the angry exodus from the car. Luckily, the map Cary drew for her told her that she was only two stops from Gerd's station. She decided to walk.

She arrived at Gerd's flat, hot and sweaty and fifteen minutes late. "I thought perhaps you'd forgotten," Gerd said when he opened his door. "Did you have trouble finding my flat?"

"No. I just ran into some trouble with the train."

"That line is always with some problem or other."

Nora made a mental note: Gerd's English was not perfect, so maybe he would tolerate her less-than-perfect German.

"I have made a pot of tea for us. Will you sit, please?"

Oh no, Nora thought, *not hot tea in this weather!* But she said, "Of course. *Danke* (thank you)."

Gerd bustled off to the kitchen to fetch the tea while Nora stood in front of an open window, piling her hair on top of her head and fanning herself with her canceled train ticket. Suddenly, she felt something hot on her bare neck. She whirled around to meet Gerd's face, inches from her own. Backing into the nearest chair, she grabbed a cup of tea from the tray Gerd had placed on a coffee table piled high with books.

"Delicious," she said as she drank the scalding tea.

"I know that many people think that it's not wise to drink hot beverages in the warm weather, but I believe it equalizes the body temperature with the air temperature, which makes one less aware of the heat outside."

"Oh yes," Nora thought, "he'd been a science teacher." His theory sounded implausible, but Gerd pronounced it with such assurance that Nora actually began to feel a little cooler.

"Are those pictures of your students?" she asked as she jumped up to get a better look at the gallery of photos framed in black on the wall facing Gerd's dining room. She moved from photo to photo, secretly hoping there might be a photo of the Nazi father in uniform. There was not. She barely had time to experience this disappointment when she felt a hand on her breast. Her instincts had been right before. Gerd *was* making a pass!

She pulled away, confused and angry. "I think I'd better be going."

"But we haven't discussed our conversation arrangements."

"I'm having second thoughts about that. Perhaps I'm not ready. Maybe I need more classes first." Nora grabbed her purse and was out the door before Gerd could respond.

"*Tschuss*! (bye-bye)" she heard him call.

"To you too, mister. I'll be damned if I'm going to put up with *that*," Nora mumbled to herself.

She'd relegated that part of her life—the sex part, as she referred to it—to a high shelf in her mind, not to be taken down and explored for a long time, perhaps never. "No Gerd or any other man is going to force me to think otherwise," she determined.

She race-walked to the nearest S-Bahn station. Thankfully, her train arrived on time. She was back at Cary's an hour later with no further mishaps.

Chapter 4

Cary was astonished when she told him what had happened at Gerd's. "I never figured him for a dirty old man," Cary said, shaking his head.

"Well, I'm not sure he is," Nora responded. "Maybe he's just lonely, or maybe I was sending him the wrong signals. I don't know, but whatever the reason, this is making me think I might just stick with classes for now."

"Meanwhile, how did you like the flat down the street?" Cary asked as he and Nora polished off the last pieces of a plum cake Monika had made before leaving for Frankfurt.

Nora chose her words carefully. "I know I could live there. It had everything I needed, but I think I'll keep looking. I think I'd like something a little bigger." (*And a little warmer and less institutional*, she added to herself.)

"I saw a sign for another holiday flat going the other way on Lichtefelde a few days ago. It's above the ice cream shop on the corner of Lichtefelde and Ostpreussendam. I think it's called '*Das Süße Leben*' (The Sweet Life). It looks from the outside like it might be a bit bigger but maybe more expensive. What do you think? Do you want to go look at it? We could walk down there for an ice cream and see if we can find someone to show it to us. Maybe the shop owner owns the flat too."

Nora was suddenly conscious of the straining waistband on her jeans. Two desserts? Every time she came to Germany, she left with four or five additional pounds. The food was so good. Germans were scornful of anything that smacked of the artificial, so fat-free and low-fat products were hard to find. Besides, she mused, all the walking she'd be doing to and from the various S-Bahn stations would melt away the pounds. "Let's go for it!"

It was a warm, sultry evening typical of late summer-early fall in Berlin. Few stores are air-conditioned in Germany, so the brisk walk and the steamy night air made cold ice cream an especially welcome treat. Sure enough, the sign for the holiday flat was still displayed in the front window of Das Süße Leben. Nora let Cary make the inquiries with a young girl behind the counter. Yes, the flat was still available. Yes, she had a key. No, the owner wasn't available, but she'd be back in the morning. Cary and Nora could take the key and let themselves into the flat. It had just been cleaned and cleared of debris from the previous tenant.

"*Danke.*" Nora accepted the key gratefully. It was a relief not to have to deal with the owner if the place turned out to be a dump. They finished their cones and sidled through the outdoor tables filled with families out for a midweek outing.

The flat's door stuck a bit, but a good shove popped it open to reveal a space straight out of "Hansel and Gretel." The walls were covered with wood paneling aged to a warm gold. A tiny table with what appeared to be a hand-embroidered tablecloth stood in the corner. A deep-red velvet couch (could it actually be Victorian?) filled out the bulk of the living room. A carved rocking chair was wedged into a corner next to the couch. Lots of pillows (also hand-embroidered?) were stacked on one end of the couch, barely concealing cushions that sagged a bit but still looked inviting. All over the walls, plaques with German sayings and small watercolors were hung at eye level.

"Wow! Talk about kitsch!" Cary exclaimed.

"I love it!" gushed Nora.

"Would you really want to live above a restaurant?" Cary asked.

"Like you did with that flat over the Indian restaurant in Schlactensee?"

"Yeah, you're right. I guess it's not really that big a problem."

Although to some, the flat looked cutesy and, as Cary termed it, kitschy. But its warmth and charm were just what Nora needed. It reached out and hugged her like a lace-collared auntie. The other flat was streamlined and efficient, but devoid of personality. In it, Nora would have felt like another stranger adrift in a culture that refused her entry. This flat oozed German *Gemultichkeit* (coziness). Mitch would have appreciated that but been appalled at all the feminine touches.

The kitchen and the bathroom didn't disappoint either. The highlight of the kitchen was a set of ceramic canisters (Nora needed to check on the freshness of the items within) labeled "flour," "salt," "coffee," "tea," and "sugar"—all in German, of course. The bathroom, although a bit musty, held all the fluffy towels and facecloths Nora would need.

"I'll take it," she told the young woman at the counter in the shop below.

"You come back tomorrow and the owner will be here. She can help you. I cannot." The young woman was more concerned about the line for cones forming behind Nora. Nora promised herself she'd come back first thing in the morning before someone else could scoop up the flat (pun intended).

The next day was to be an important one. Monika was returning from her business trip. Nora and Monika had become friends as well as sisters-in-law, but Nora's last visit had tested their friendship. Nora and Mitch had "house-sat" for Monika and Cary. Nora thought she was being helpful when she cleaned the house from top to bottom. She even hand-washed Monika's tiny car, one of the first Mercedes-Benz "smart cars." But Nora was afraid that Monika had interpreted this cleaning spree as a criticism of her own housekeeping, and Nora had to admit, several things *had* gotten broken during their stay in the house.

After expressing nominal thanks for Nora's efforts, Monika had bustled about rearranging the rearranged furniture, repairing the damage to a broken blind in the den, and mending tears in the screens where Meister, the cat, had slipped in and out of the house before Mitch noticed the damage.

Monika's response had puzzled Nora. She loved Monika. She and Monika had shared many soulful conversations about their goals in life, their concerns about their children (Monika had a fourteen-year-old son, Florian, from her first marriage), and their worries about their aging parents. Nora had assumed they shared the same values when it came to maintaining a house.

But this was Monika's first house. Even as a child, she'd always lived in flats. Her first house represented something she'd never thought she'd achieve in her lifetime. Most people in Germany— roughly 60 percent, according to statistics—rent rather than own property, be it a flat or a house. There's no stigma associated with renting in Germany, as there is in the US. Monika's house was infused with her personality, but the purchase itself was due to Cary's influence. Nora remembered when, a few weeks before their move into the house, Monika confessed to her that she was a little fearful about taking possession of the house. "Who will be there if we have a problem? The neighbors have their own houses to look after. I will miss having people on the other side of a wall. I will be lonely."

This was before the new neighborhood won her over. There were plenty of young families on their street, including a German-American family living across from Cary and Monika. Dave and Ingrid Hochsteller were Cary and Monika's best friends from the start. Dave came from Idaho, Ingrid from just outside Stuttgart. Their five sons were all born in Europe but traveled to the US every summer to "explore their American side," as Ingrid expressed it.

Mitch had assured Nora that Monika's brusqueness would pass with time, but Nora was nervous about reconnecting with Monika. Would Monika welcome her with open arms as she had in the past, or would the tension from the previous visit color this visit too? Nora had not talked to Cary about her misgivings because she didn't want to put him in the middle. She felt a little resentful about withholding her fears from Cary. She was used to telling Cary everything.

Nora and Cary had shared so many adventures. Before Cary's marriage, he and Nora traveled together more often than Nora and Mitch. She secretly believed that Mitch had been a little jealous of her relationship with Cary, although she herself was a bit jealous of Monika, whom she suspected had replaced her in Cary's affections.

Chapter 5

Cary had a full day of classes, so Nora volunteered to pick up Monika at the airport. She carefully backed Monika's car out of the driveway and through the front gate. Her first stop was at Das Süße Leben to talk to the owner of the holiday flat she'd fallen in love with the night before. An older woman around Nora's age with a tight crop of silver curls was stationed behind the cash register.

"*Guten Tag*," said Nora. "Sprechen Sie English, bitte?"

"Yes, a little."

"My name is Nora Reinhart. I was here last night to look at your flat upstairs. I would like to rent it if it's still available." Nora's fingers were crossed behind her back, a habit from childhood.

"I am Ilsa Meijer. I am the owner of this shop and of the flat. No, it has not been rented. Some people have expressed interest, but no one has made a deposit. The rent is six hundred euros a month. How long would you want the flat?"

"Three months. I'd like to make a deposit now and possibly move in this week."

"Good, very good. The deposit will be the first month's rent."

"Can I give you a hundred euros now and come back tomorrow with the rest of the money?"

"Ya, sure."

Nora handed over nearly all of the euros in her purse and left the shop delighting in her good fortune at finding a flat that suited her so well. This would be the first place she had lived in without a family member, friend, or spouse. It felt dangerously exhilarating.

More dangerous and far less exhilarating was the drive to Tegel. Nora was not a fast driver, and going over the metric equivalent of sixty miles an hour made her very nervous. She struggled to keep pace with the other cars on the inter-city autobahn. She had memorized all the German road signs from a website but was having trouble distinguishing one from another. Several drivers passed her, blowing their horns as they flew by. They had little tolerance for a driver who ventured onto the autobahn yet seemed so tenuous about speed.

Miraculously, she arrived at Tegel with a half hour to spare. She found a parking spot in an out-of-the-way lot behind the airport. Now if I can just remember where I parked, she thought. She found Monika's gate and waited.

Monika burst through the gate—in a hurry, as always. "Nora!" she cried and wrapped her arms around Nora. "It is so good to see you! I am so happy you came to see us again." She pulled away to scan Nora's face anxiously. "Are you OK? I am so sorry we couldn't come to the funeral. Do you miss him terribly? He was such a good man. I liked him so very much." Monika's words tumbled out, her soft breathy voice hitting the right notes of love and concern.

"Yes, I miss him, but I'm determined to get on with my life. I have to learn to live on my own. I haven't done that for many, many years, you know."

"I know that, but you must allow yourself to feel sad. We will help you with all the rest," Monika assured Nora.

With an enormous sense of relief, Nora recognized the old Monika, the one with whom she made an instant connection when they first met. When she first met Monika, Nora and Cary were at a bar where some of the members of the English-speakers club Cary helped start were gathered. Cary was describing his dating misadventures in Germany. He had even tried speed dating, but his less-than-speedy German made the five-minute encounters with prospective dates nearly useless. "I wanted to tell them that my German makes me sound like a fifth grader, but I'm really a very well-educated person," Cary confessed to the group gathered at a big round table in the middle of the bar.

A lovely woman with dark brown hair and a wonderful smile walked into the bar, obviously looking for someone. "Is this the Connections group?" she asked Cary.

"Yes, it is. I'm Cary and this is my sister Nora, and there's . . ." Cary's introductions traveled around the table with a flurry of "hello's" and "welcomes."

"I am Monika Neiderlander. I read about this group on your website. I studied German in the US, but I don't have a chance to speak it much here in Berlin."

The evening passed uneventfully with drinks and jokes and promises to meet again soon. Cary and Nora rose to walk to the S-Bahn station. "Would you like a ride?" Monika asked. She dropped them off at a station halfway to Cary's flat in Schlactensee, not too far from Monika's own flat.

"You know, Cary," Nora later mused, "she would be perfect for you."

Nora repeated this story often as if she had been the first to predict Cary and Monika's union, even crediting herself with being a matchmaker for the pair, although her role in their coming together had really been minimal.

The ride back to Cary's with Monika was quiet, both women lost in their own thoughts. Nora was dreaming about life in her new flat, conjuring up small dinner parties with her handful of German acquaintances (not including the errant Gerd). She even went so far as to plan the menu for her first soiree. "Should I go German or American?" she mused.

Monika's thoughts traveled a different route. She tried to imagine what it would be like to lose Cary. She had waited so many years to find someone like him. How could she survive without him? She was only married to Florian's father a few years before they divorced amidst a host of ugly recriminations. She essentially raised Florian alone. His father, Wolfgang, had little interest in the boy, and relations between Cary and Florian were a little strained. Cary had a hard time resisting the temptation to lecture, and Florian didn't see much in his new American stepfather to pique his interest. Nevertheless, Cary had proved to be a very satisfying sounding board for Monika's concerns about her high-spirited son.

"Stop worrying," Monika said to herself. "Cary is young. He's healthy and, most important, he is totally loyal," she assured herself. She had no reason to fear he'd leave her—for whatever reason—anytime soon. But still she worried. It was her nature.

Chapter 6

Nora's move to her holiday flat took next to no time. She didn't have much to take with her other than her clothes and a stack of books. The flat was equipped with almost everything she needed to cook simple meals and spend cozy nights deciphering German TV or reading her meager supply of novels. She stood in her tiny living room and assessed the terrain. As an amateur interior designer, she sensed the layout needed a little tweaking. She slid the couch a foot to the right to give someone sitting in the rocker more rocking space. She was dismayed by the large stain on the newly exposed section of carpet. It looked suspiciously like blood. She resisted the temptation to sniff the offending spot and slid the couch back to its previous place. "Why borrow trouble," she told herself.

No matter how she rearranged the furniture, there always seemed to be something the old arrangement hid—a stain, a hole in the baseboard (a mouse hole?), a missing piece of molding, a dent in the wall (had someone kicked it?). It was clear the furniture had been strategically placed to camouflage these flaws. "So much for putting my stamp on the place," Nora thought. A few family photos and her books lined up on a lone shelf might have to suffice for personalizing the flat.

She stood in the doorway to the bathroom and scanned the living room again. A colorful throw and new inserts for the charming but deflated pillows could make a world of difference. Nora resolved to hit her favorite stores in the morning. Shopping in Germany was one of her favorite pastimes, and although she needed no specific reason to shop, this time she would be on a mission. She knew exactly where she'd find the items she wanted.

What Nora really needed—but was reluctant to admit to herself—was something to do. While surveying her new flat, she tried to ignore the nagging voice within that accused her of having no real purpose for this time in Berlin.

"All right," she said aloud to silence the voice that sounded a lot like her dead mother's. "I'll check into taking another class in the morning." She snuggled into the corner of her sofa, trying to coax the flat pillows into a cushy backrest, and opened the book at the top of her stack.

Nora was well aware that she needed to read slowly since she only had a few books with her. Books in English were very expensive in Europe. She could quickly eat a hole in her budget if she bought too many. "Find a good used bookstore," she added to her mental list of errands. Signing up for a class, decorating the flat, stocking her new kitchen—these were probably not endeavors that would help uncover a purpose for this stay in Germany, but since she had yet to identify her goal, these errands would help keep at bay what she termed "the lonelies." And maybe after all, that *was* her goal.

Nora sensed that activity was crucial to avoid dealing with anything disturbing. "I don't want to think about things right now," she thought with the mental equivalent of stamping her foot, as the edge of a dark thought crept into her consciousness.

German television could always provide a distraction. Although Nora struggled to understand the dialogue, the story lines were usually familiar. Many German dramas seemed to be based on the novels of the British romance writer Rosamunde Pilcher. They were family sagas where the question of who fathered whom seemed to be at the core of many conflicts. There were also plenty of *Crimis*,

German whodunits. Nora's favorite was *Der Dicke* (the fat one) whose hero was a lawyer who struggled with both his weight and his unruly office staff of three prickly women: his partner, their secretary, and the office cleaning woman. Despite his size—at least three hundred pounds on a six-foot frame—the hero had a sexy quality that emanated from his deep, throaty voice.

Nora dozed off and woke a few hours later with a sore neck and cold feet. "Got to get that throw and do something about these pillows," she resolved. She unpacked one of the oversized T-shirts she always slept in and trudged off to her somewhat lumpy bed, sure she wouldn't sleep a wink. But hours later, the sliver of sunshine peeking through the bedroom blinds told her she had indeed slept—and much longer than she'd planned to.

She consulted the big book of Berlin train, tram, and bus routes and decided that her best bet was a bus that took her into the nearby shopping area of Zehlendorf. Within the four blocks of Zehlendorf's retail center, there were at least six women's clothing stores, several small department stores, a big *Backerei* (bakery), a mini-Burger King, three good *Doner/* kebab stands, and the Zehlendorf Rathaus (town hall).

The *Rathskeller* in the basement of the Rathaus was where city employees and penny-pinching senior citizens ate, although the lunch crowd was usually just nine or ten "over-seventies." (Nora felt like a kid!) There was always a big kettle of the day's stew (veggies and an assortment of some unknown meat) as well as a pot of the soup du jour.

Nora was hooked on the soups at the Rathaus Rathskeller. So much so, in fact, that on previous trips, the chef had often tried to persuade Nora to order something other than soup. "*Immer mit die Suppe,*" (always with the soup) he'd say after she loaded her bowl with bean (*Bohnen*) or vegetable (*Gemüse*) soup. A tall Coca-Cola on the side, and she got away for under four euros. As she walked down the street toward the Rathaus, Nora could almost taste the salty, slightly briny broth of the vegetable soup the Rathskeller was famous for. "Lunch first, shop after," she told herself.

She was dismayed to find that the Rathskeller had been remodeled. It was still in the basement of the city hall, but it had a shiny new look and a new menu to match. Gone were the savory soups and stews. They were replaced by tacos, empanadas, and "sliders"—the greasy mini-burgers Nora particularly disliked. The prices were still cheaper than in most other Zehlendorf restaurants, so Nora settled into a spot at a long communal table next to a man a few years older than her.

"You must go up to the counter to order your food," he said in halting German.

"Do you speak English?" Nora replied in German (one of the few German sentences that rolled easily off her tongue).

"Yes, better than my German."

"Do you come from Berlin?"

"No, I come from Liege in Wallonia."

"Where is Wallonia?" Nora asked. The moment the words slipped out, she was embarrassed at her ignorance. "Dumb American," she said to herself.

"Wallonia is the French-speaking part of Belgium."

"Ooh, my French is even worse than my German! What brings you to Berlin?"

"My sister lived in Berlin. I came to visit her in the hospital, but I arrived too late. She passed away before I could get here." Sadness and remorse were etched in the deep lines on his long slim face and in his pale blue eyes.

"I'm so sorry to hear that. Please accept my condolences," Nora said formally, unsure of how to respond to this frank expression of grief. "My name is Nora Reinhart," she added quickly. "I'm here for a few months on sabbatical from my college in the United States," Nora volunteered. Then she wondered if it was wise to offer so much information to a stranger, even though it seemed only fair after his revelation.

"I too will be here for some time. I need to settle my sister's estate. Her husband had already died and they had no children, so there is no one else to do it."

"May I ask your name?"

"Oh, excuse me. I am not myself these days. My name is Guy Guzman, Madame Reinhart," he added, tipping an imaginary hat, a tiny smile lifting the corners of his thin-drawn mouth. Guy was one of those lucky older men who still had a full head of hair. Silvery gray, swept back from his temples, he was the picture of aging elegance. Nora secretly compared him to Mitch who was pleasant-looking enough but anything but elegant.

"Please, call me Nora. May I call you Guy?"

Now it was Guy's turn to be taken aback. *Americans are always so casual*, he mused, remembering another American from his days in the Architecture Department at the University of Liege.

"Of course, but I must tell you that I may slip occasionally and call you 'Madame Reinhart.' It's an old man's habit. After seventy years, it's hard to break the customs of one's youth. So, you are a professor?" Guy asked, changing the subject so rapidly, Nora caught her breath.

"Uh, yes, yes, I am. I teach full-time at my college—really a small university—in the Midwestern part of the US, in the Communication Department."

"And what sort of communication do you teach?" Guy asked with the smallest hint of a twinkle in his eye. Nora wasn't sure how to answer this.

"It's all about how people relate to each other in their conversations—what they say to their spouse, for example, or even what's said on TV or in a movie." Nora sensed that this clumsy response did little to explain the vast, complex field of study she'd loved for over thirty years.

She took another stab at it, launching into something that felt a little like her lectures in COMM 101. Guy seemed interested, sprinkling questions here and there to encourage her. The next thing Nora knew, the room was growing darker and the kitchen staff seemed to be making noises that usually signal the desire to close up shop.

"Oh my gosh," explained Nora. "It's almost five. Why did you let me go on and on? I'm really sorry. That was so rude of me."

"Not at all," Guy assured her. "It was a pleasure to hear someone speak so eloquently about their academic discipline."

"But I don't know anything about *you*. You must tell me all about yourself sometime. But right now, I have to go. I'm due at my brother's for dinner to celebrate my sister-in-law's homecoming."

"I will look forward to sharing my field with you the next time we meet," Guy said, sliding back his chair and gathering up a small cache of canvas bags.

"Oh my gosh," Nora said again. "I was supposed to bring the wine for dinner. It's too late to stop at a wine store. I need to catch the bus back, and my bus only runs every twenty minutes."

"Please, let me give you a ride. We can stop at a little shop I know on Annaliese Strasse. It's not far from here."

On impulse, Nora agreed. When Guy dropped her off at Cary's, she acted on another impulse. "Would you like to come to my flat for dinner this week? How about Friday night?"

Guy shook his head delightedly. "You Americans don't waste too much time, do you? Of course I'll come. Or as they say here in Germany, *ya, Gerne.*"

Chapter 7

"**N**ora, what were you thinking? You don't know this person. Do you really think it's wise to have him in your flat alone? What happens if he makes a play for you like Gerd did?" Cary was full of objections, but Nora sensed Guy was nothing like Gerd. For one thing, his obvious grief over the loss of his sister gave him a wistful—no, *careful*—quality. She suspected that she and Guy shared a similar instinct to protect themselves against further loss.

Besides, a dinner party would give Nora a chance to resurrect her cooking skills. It had been so long since she'd cooked a meal for anyone. Before Mitch died, their meals together had dwindled to clear broths, and occasionally, when Mitch felt stronger than usual, thin slices of homemade bread from a local bakery. Mitch developed a love of ice-cream bars near the end, and Nora found herself constantly replenishing their supply when Mitch ate two, even three, a day. She never wanted to see another frozen Dove bar again!

Monika was also skeptical about Nora's first guest, but allowed for the possibility that Guy might fill a void for Nora. Not the void left by Mitch, but the void left in the life of a woman used to students, colleagues, friends, and yes, even children—even though Nora's were grown. Monika knew that even though Nora fancied herself a woman of intellect, a large part of Nora defined herself in terms of her relationships. A new relationship might be just what Nora needed, Monika mused.

"I'm not looking for anything romantic," Nora said, almost in response to Monika's unspoken thoughts. "Guy just lost his sister. He seems to need someone to talk to or, in my case, someone to listen to," she added, chagrined. She had to make a point to draw out Guy, to find out what interested *him*. No more intellectual monologues from her.

"Are you sure you don't want us to drop by? We could simply 'be in the neighborhood.'" asked Cary.

"You *are* in the neighborhood. No, don't worry. I can take care of myself. I'll send you a text if things get out of hand."

"That might be too late. You're not exactly a whiz at texting."

"Neither are you, my friend."

"OK, you two." Monika held up a hand. "Stop. I need to get up in the morning and get back to the office. Cary, you have a 9:00 a.m. class. And, Nora . . ."

"*I* have nothing in the morning. Oh wait, yes I do. I never actually went shopping yesterday. I got so caught up talking to Guy. I have stuff to buy!" she added gaily.

"Go to it, girl," said Cary as he kissed her goodnight. She walked the four blocks to her flat, planning her menu for Friday night. Nora smiled. Got to include ice cream!

*   *   *

"But why does she not seem sad?" Monika asked Cary at breakfast the next morning.

"Because she won't let herself feel sad," he explained. "It's been that way ever since I can remember. When our folks died in that car crash, Nora bustled around—calling caterers for the wake, buying a new suit for Mitch, even having her hair done. I don't believe she's dealt with Mom and Dad's deaths even now. I worry that when she does start to feel things—and I'm willing to bet it'll be soon—it'll be like Hoover Dam bursting."

"What is Hoover Dam?"

"I don't have time to explain it now. Just know that it will be really awful."

"But if she doesn't let herself feel things, why did she always seem so angry with Mitch?"

"I'm not sure. Maybe anger is really another kind of sadness."

Nora did seem to have a special ability to shut out the bad stuff—at least on a conscious level. But the iron will that held her emotions in check in the daytime was far less effective at night. Ever since that awful day in the oncologist's office when they were told Mitch had only a few months left, Nora struggled with night demons. Facing the loss of her husband brought back all her earlier losses.

She believed that she rarely slept, but when she did, her dreams were filled with screams and shattered glass. She often caught glimpses of her mother's gray hair, matted with blood, and her father's swollen hand. In recent months, she had turned to Mitch for comfort—only to find him struggling for breath, trying unsuccessfully to keep a persistent cough from waking her.

She never shared her dreams with anyone, even though Mitch pleaded with her to see a therapist. "That's just your way of washing your hands of me, foisting me off on a therapist," she would fume.

When Mitch died, her dreams took a different turn. Now her dreams often placed her on a narrow precipice overlooking a deep crevasse. She had a terrible fear of heights, and this fear hit her full force in her dreams. She would wake to find herself, T-shirt soaked to the skin, shaking from a horror she couldn't quite identify. She remembered her dream self thinking "I know I'm going to fall. I may as well jump. Why prolong the agony?"

Although she couldn't pinpoint the source of her fears, Nora knew when they began. Years before, Cary had been a ranger at Glacier National Park in Montana. At his urging, Nora agreed to join a hike he was leading on the park's High Line Trail. The walk began in a lovely meadow filled with the vivid red wildflowers called "Paint Brush." After a short drop, the trail snaked along the side of a mountain. The path was narrow and slippery from a recent rain. In some spots, the trail was so narrow that some considerate soul had attached a long length of garden hose to the mountainside as a handhold. Her friend Cele walked ahead of her. Nora carefully placed each foot in Cele's footsteps, not allowing herself to look up, down, or to the left where the valley below yawned. Suddenly, Cele stopped and turned to Nora. "Do you want to go back?" she asked.

"Oh my god, yes," breathed Nora.

Mitch was several hikers ahead and, at the sound of Nora's voice, he too turned and saw Nora and Cele frozen in place. He inched back and took each by the hand, and together, the three made their slow, careful way back to the meadow. She had never felt as grateful to anyone as she did to Mitch that day. But instead of thanking him, she accused him of thinking she was weak. "I could have made it without you, you know. You don't always have to rescue me." Mitch had stalked away. He was determined to catch up with Cary and the other hikers to finish the walk that ended with a spectacular view of a sparkling lake nestled in a ring of tall scrub pines.

When Nora thought about that day, her stomach still flipped at the thought of the drop to the valley below the trail. She knew in her heart that she should have echoed the thanks Cele lavished on Mitch. But as long as Cele expressed her gratitude, why should she? It only gave a man like Mitch—with his supreme sense of self-confidence—even more power over her, she reasoned.

Nora shook her head vigorously to shake off the memories. She had an outfit to pick out and a dinner to prepare, even though she assured herself this dinner with Guy was not a date. It was simply an evening with a new friend. It was important to Nora to convey that message to Guy with what she wore. She dug among her meager travel clothes and settled on a sleeveless black crepe shell, a black-and-white flowered skirt, and her only pair of black sandals—a bit clunky for evening wear, but they would have to do. Besides, they reinforced a "no nonsense" message to Guy, should he attempt something similar to Gerd's aborted pass.

A few hours later, when the rich scent of beef stew perfumed the little flat, a timid knock shook the front door. Guy stood on her doorstep with a huge bouquet of lilies nearly blocking a view of his face.

"Guy?"

"Yes, it is me, come with an entire bower of flowers for you."

Nora giggled. "I think the word 'bower' is only used to refer to trees or bushes," the professor in her corrected.

"Something smells wonderful. Is that *beef bourguignon*?"

"No, it's just plain old American beef stew, but I added a little red wine to the sauce to give it some zing."

"Well, I look forward to tasting this 'zing.'"

Nora settled comfortably into the role of the grand dame. Before he got sick, she and Mitch had entertained often; and despite its small size and the unpretentious atmosphere of her German flat, Nora's natural sense of style kicked in. Guy had brought a bottle of a deep dark Merlot, so they savored a glass before settling in at the tiny dining room table.

After the first few bites of stew, Nora said, "Please tell me all about yourself. I told you about me when we met at the Rathaus, now I want to hear all about *you*."

"Well, as I told you before, I grew up in Liege. I went to university in Paris, and then returned to Liege to work as an architect for an international firm with their headquarters in Liege. My wife and I were married there and had a house just outside Liege for many years. She died a few years ago from ovarian cancer."

"Do you still have family in Liege?"

"No, my sister was all the family I had left. My sister and I lived with an aunt in Liege but she died many years ago after we had both grown up."

"What about your parents?"

Guy's eyes clouded over. "My parents died in Auschwitz. My ancestors were originally Sephardic Jews from Spain but, like many others, they sought refuge in Belgium. My parents met in Brussels and moved to Liege together."

"But how were you and your sister saved, or am I asking too many personal questions?"

"It's all right. This all happened so many years ago. My parents were hearing rumors about the fate of Jews in Europe even in the mid-1930s. So early in the war, they arranged for my sister Lillet and me to go to live with a family in Sweden. We lived with the Runeberg family for eight years. I was nine years old when we returned to Belgium. My aunt Aimee had lived in the United States for many years, but she too returned to Belgium after the war to take care of my sister and I."

"Were the Runebergs kind to you and Lillet?"

"They took good care of us, but they were not warm people. They provided food and shelter and sent my sister and I to a good school, but I don't think any love ever developed in them for us. Mr. Runeberg had met my father at an international architecture conference in the 1920s, and they became fast friends. When my father asked him to take us in during the war, Mr. Runeberg reluctantly agreed. You see, the Runebergs were not Jewish, and even though they were good people, they had some typical feelings about Jews."

"Like what?"

"Oh, I can't really say. All I know comes from my aunt, and she only found out a little bit about what had happened with us from a neighbor of my parents when she returned to Belgium. So much of this could be wrong. I just don't know. People don't seem to want to talk about what went on with the Jews during the war. There is a sort of 'code of silence' about these things."

"And your aunt—was she good to you?"

"My Aunt Aimee was well-named. Her name is very close to the French verb for 'to love'—*aimer*. She was only twenty-eight years old when she returned to Belgium, but she took on the role of mother without hesitation. After we returned to Belgium, Lillet and I had a very peaceful and loving childhood in spite of the loss of our parents. You see, I was a baby when we went to live with the Runebergs, and Lillet was only five years old. Obviously, I never knew my parents, and Lillet barely remembered them. Aimee was all a mother should be. I loved her more than I've ever loved anyone in my life, except for Lillet."

Nora was puzzled about what might have happened to Guy's wife and why he hadn't mentioned her when he spoke about his love for his aunt and his sister. But she felt she had probed his history for as much information as he felt comfortable giving, so she returned to the safer topic of her research in Berlin.

"I've forgotten to mention the official purpose of this trip for me," Nora said, shifting to her professor persona. "Since this is actually a research sabbatical, I am expected to do some actual research. I am interested in the process of storytelling, especially the everyday stories people tell that suggest how they feel about a subject and the unique perspectives these stories reveal. I plan to explore the concept of 'victimage' in the stories former East Germans tell about life before and after reunification versus the stories former West Germans tell. I've heard a number of these stories from German friends in casual conversations. My research project will place these stories in a theoretical framework." Nora hoped she didn't sound too pompous and pedantic.

"I had originally planned on using my sister-in-law as my interpreter. My German is way too basic for interviewing Germans on a topic this sensitive. But Monika now has a new job working for the Technical University here, so she doesn't have time to help. I considered hiring a student or maybe just being very selective with my interviewees, talking only with people with a good command of English. I haven't made up my mind yet on exactly how I'll handle this."

"Perhaps I can help. I have business here in Berlin with my sister's estate as I told you before, but that won't take much of my time. My German is rusty, but it's coming back to me. Could you use an old man as your volunteer interpreter?"

"But don't you have to get back to work in Liege?"

"I am what they refer to in Germany as *ein Pensionar*, what you call in English 'a retiree.' I give an occasional lecture at the university in Liege and I write a bit, but the writing I can do anywhere. Besides, I too am curious about these stories. I have few friends in Germany, so it would be nice to meet more Germans personally. The only Germans I talk with regularly are Lillet's housekeeper, the baker in my *Backerei* in Zehlendorf, and the man who sells me my monthly train pass."

"Well, if you don't think you'd be too bored, I think I'll take you up on your offer. Shake?" Nora stuck out her hand.

"Shake!" said Guy with perhaps more enthusiasm than the venture warranted.

"Now, I suggest we take advantage of my sweet neighbor downstairs and go down and have some ice cream. What do you think?"

Accidentally on purpose, they met Cary and Monika at the entrance to Das Süße Leben. "Fancy meeting you here," said Cary.

"That's something Americans say when they want you to think you're meeting them by accident, but it's really on purpose," Nora confided to Guy. "Guy, this is my brother Cary and his wife, Monika. Cary and Monika, this is my friend Guy Guzman."

Cary grabbed Guy's hand, pumping it vigorously. Monika blinked several times. "Nora, can I see you upstairs for a minute?"

"Sure. We were just about to go in for some ice cream. Cary, maybe you and Guy can find us a table."

Nora followed Monika as she bounded up the stairs. She could hardly contain herself as Nora struggled with the door to her flat. "Nora, do you have any idea who that is?" Monika asked when they were inside. "Guy Guzman is one of the most famous architects in Europe. He is as well known in Europe as Frank Lloyd Wright in the United States. He has designed many famous buildings in Belgium as well as the main assembly hall of the European Parliament building in Brussels."

"Wow! And he's going to help me with my study! This is going to be so great!" Nora enthused as she reached for the doorknob.

"Wait," Monika grabbed Nora's arm. "There's more. He was arrested for murder several years ago. I don't remember the details, but it was quite a scandal at the time."

"Murder?" Nora asked incredulously, well aware of Monika's flair for the dramatic.

"Well, maybe not murder. I don't think the man actually died, but there *were* accusations. Anyway, you really must be careful. He may be dangerous."

"I hardly think so," Nora scoffed, recalling the shadow of grief in Guy's eyes. "But I'll get on the Internet and 'google' him. I'm sure there'll be plenty of information. The Internet has information on *everybody*. Come on. Let's go downstairs. I want to make sure Guy is really up for my project."

"Nora, you are either very brave or very foolish," Monika said, shaking her head in disbelief.

"Probably a little of both."

Cary and Guy were deep in conversation. It turned out that Cary had seen several of the buildings Guy designed and had lots of questions about form and function and Guy's choice of building materials. Guy revealed that he had a weakness for stone.

"Its subtle color variations can convey so many moods, but always, there is a tranquility about stone," Guy was saying.

He stood when Nora and Monika joined them at the table. "Cary, we must go now," Monika urged him. "I got a call from Florian while we were upstairs. He needs to be picked up at the Lankwitz station."

"Oh, he can wait a few minutes. We were in the middle of something here."

"No, Cary, we must go right now." Something in Monika's tone told Cary that she was not to be put off. "OK, OK. I hope to see you again sometime, Guy. I enjoyed our conversation," Cary said as he rose. Monika was already out the door and headed for their car.

"I as well," called Guy. He turned to Nora. "She told you, didn't she?"

"I'm not sure what you mean." Nora couldn't meet Guy's gaze. "Monika was just concerned about her son. She's a tad overprotective." The lie slid off her tongue unconvincingly.

"Nora, something happened about ten years ago—"

Nora cut him off. "I don't need to know whatever it is. We both probably have things we'd rather not talk about. I know I do.

Let's get our ice cream. I have the first interview for my research in the morning, and I need to get up early to get to Mitte by nine o'clock."

"Shall I come and translate for you?" Guy asked.

"No, this person speaks English. I'll call you later in the week when I've scheduled some interviews with people who speak only German."

They ate their ice cream in silence. A short while later, Guy's tiny VW Lupo pulled away. Their evening ended on a sour note.

Chapter 8

Nora's first interview was with Marta, Monika's best friend. Nora met Marta in the café at the big Hugendubel on the KuDamm, not far from Nora's favorite department store, *Kaufhaus den Western* (Department Store of the West), also known as KaDeWe. Marta grew up in what had been West Germany. Marta saw herself as having taken a personal political stand against the oppression of the "Ossies" in Communist East Germany (the "GDR"). On impulse, she'd agreed to marry a man from East Berlin she'd never met who wanted to come to the West for a university education. In East Germany, he'd been assigned to work on the Bahn system, but he aspired to something more intellectual. After the wedding, there was no pretense about the union being anything more than a political gesture. Marta and her ex-husband never lived together. Once he'd moved to West Berlin to be with his "wife," the liaison ended.

"It seemed a very exciting and brave adventure at the time," she said. But years later, she confessed to Nora, she was appalled by such "recklessness." A few months after their divorce, Marta saw her former husband on the KuDamm. They barely spoke.

The day the Wall came down, Marta was riding on the U-Bahn when she noticed many people "with really bad jeans" and "terrible shoes." She later found out they were residents of East Berlin who had streamed into the West on that remarkable day in 1989. At the time, she was rooming with several Iranian students near the Technical University in Berlin. Her roommates were scared, reluctant to leave the flat because they mistakenly thought the "Ossies" were Nazis.

At home, Nora tried to transcribe her notes from the interview with Marta, but her thoughts kept straying to Guy. Her sensible self told her to beware of Guy. He could be dangerous. But the part of herself that loved a good mystery encouraged her to contact Guy and see what develops. "But if you arrange to meet again, make it in a public place," her sensible side counseled.

But if she did meet him again, should she find out exactly what he'd done, or was the subject best left alone? Nora simply couldn't make up her mind. She struggled to unravel her thoughts from the tangle of Guy's sketchy past. One day, she would put aside her reservations and vow to call him the next day. But when the next day came, she concluded that any contact with Guy was foolhardy and promised herself to wipe him from her thoughts.

Almost two weeks passed with this mental tug-of-war. Nora completed several more interviews, but her heart wasn't really in the project. "All right. That's it," she told herself one rainy morning. "I'm calling him."

Guy was pleasant enough on the phone, but Nora sensed a slight chilliness in his tone. Could it be that *he* had reservations about *her*? That seemed so unlikely, she put it out of her mind. She told Guy that she had scheduled her first interview with a German-only speaker, Cary and Monika's neighbor, Anya. They arranged to meet in the morning at Nora's flat where she'd have strong American coffee waiting. Guy promised to bring croissants from his neighborhood *Backarei*. Nora hung up, wishing she had said something reassuring to Guy, something that could wipe the slate clean of any lingering suspicions she had of him (or that he may have of her).

She tossed and turned that night in her narrow little bed. She hated the way German beds were made with the big flat Euro pillow that she never could seem to fold in a proper roll to wedge under her neck. The floppy German duvet always started out cool and smooth, but eventually felt hot and bulky. She could seldom manage to keep her feet tucked under the duvet that constantly slipped off the bed. And after several nights of dreamless sleep, her nightmares were back in full force.

Nora finally gave up at five o'clock, determined to finish an article on German reunification she'd been promising herself she'd read. It had languished on her tiny kitchen table, calling out to her for days. She managed to get through the first half of the article when she heard a soft knock on her front door. She sat bolt upright. Should she answer the door or pretend to be asleep?

Nora peeked around the front window. Ilsa Meijer, her landlady, stood on her doorstep, shivering a bit in the early morning chill. "Ilsa?" Nora asked with a degree of alarm. "Are you OK?"

"Oh yes. I am fine. I saw your light and wondered if *you* were all right."

"I'm fine too," Nora said with relief. "I was just having trouble sleeping, so I decided to get up and read a bit."

"That also happens to me often. Would you like to join me for a cup of tea while I open the shop?"

"You open your ice cream shop this early?"

"Oh, we serve breakfast too. Not a lot—just *Brotchen* and fruit, but we have several people in the neighborhood that come every day before work. Not many. Really not even enough to make it profitable to open this early, but I am used to them and they count on me, so I open each weekday at seven."

"Just let me throw on some clothes and I'll come down and join you."

"'Throw on clothes'? What does that mean?"

Nora laughed. "It's just an American expression that means putting on one's clothes quickly."

Downstairs, a small group had gathered at a large round table near the kitchen. Four middle-aged men dressed in suits and two younger women dressed in what passed in Berlin as "office casual" (black jeans, black T's, black sneakers, and black hoodies). Ilsa made introductions, adding "Herr" or "Frau" to each last name.

"Hi! I'm Nora Reinhart," she said quickly before Ilsa could tack a "Frau" onto *her* last name. The young women looked amused by Nora's informality. The men seemed shocked. Nora interpreted their reaction as "Moving to the 'du' so soon?"

"I'll only be here a few months, so I'd like to get to know you all a little quicker than I usually would," she explained, hoping this rationale would be sufficient reason to bypass the normal German progression from the formal "Sie" acquaintance to the casual, friends, and family "du."

This was not the way things were done in Germany though, except among members of the younger generation. As she always did, Nora assumed others would make an exception for her. All her life, she had flashed a dimpled smile while pushing aside the rules everyone else lived by. She had her own set of far more rigorous rules.

"Wo kommen Sie?" (Where do you come from?) said one of the men, refusing to buy into Nora's get-to-know-you ploy. This was also his way of letting her know that she was in Germany, where people spoke German.

"Ich komme aus den Vereiningung Staten," (I come from the United States.) Nora responded, to prove that she could speak German but simply preferred English.

One of the two young women answered enthusiastically in English. "Do you live anywhere near Chicago? I went there last year to visit my aunt."

"So this is the way it'll be," Nora thought. "I'll speak English with the women and German with the men." She recalled Cary's speed-dating dilemma. "I wonder how I can explain to them that even though I sound like a ten-year-old in German, I'm actually a professor with a PhD." She was surprised she hadn't been able to sweetly bulldoze her way into a more casual conversation with the older men.

Nora had arrived just as most of the others were about to leave. Several told her they needed to catch a bus into Zehlendorf that stopped at the corner across from Ilsa's shop. *"Bis Spater"* (See you later), Nora said to the backs of the four men.

"We don't need to leave yet," said Katja, the young woman who had visited Chicago. "We both work in the office building across the street, so we have lots of time. The men that were here work in Zehlendorf at the big Siemens building," she informed Nora. "Tell us why you're here in Berlin," she said with a sniff that implied that no one in their right mind would leave the US to visit Germany.

"I am officially here to do some research. I'm a professor in the United States."

"I was a student here at Freie University, but I stopped going to classes. I don't like school very much," Paula, Katya's friend confessed.

"University is not for everyone. I've had many students who probably should have gone from high school to a job or some sort of vocational program. The academic environment wasn't a good 'fit' for them."

"'Fit?' Like when shoes feel good on your feet?"

Nora was again reminded that just knowing how to speak another language didn't mean that one understood all the nuances of that language. She remembered a funny conversation with Monika in which she tried to explain the difference between "strict" and "inflexible."

Katya glanced casually at the clock face on her "handy" (what Germans call their cell phones), then leapt out of her chair, sucking down the last of her apple juice. "Paula, we have to go. It's almost nine!" The two girls ran out together, calling their good-byes to Nora. *"Tsusch* (bye)! See you soon!"

"Oh my gosh," Nora said to herself. "Guy will be here soon, and I'm not dressed properly." She somehow knew that Guy would expect to see her in professional dress even though their interview would be little more than a casual conversation with Cary's neighbor, Anna, with whom Nora had developed a relationship during her previous visit to Berlin.

Guy arrived fifteen minutes later. Nora had just enough time to pull a comb through her hair after "throwing on" her black dress pants and a crisp white shirt. Guy had not only brought croissants, but a pudding made of *Quark* and cherries. Nora luckily had the foresight to ask Ilsa for a fresh pot of coffee. Not American, of course, but rich and dark and flavored with just a hint of caramel. Although Nora was not at all hungry after munching on her favorite *Sonnenblumen Brotchen* (a small roll with sunflowers seeds) with the breakfast group, she forced down a croissant. She politely refused the Quark. She had never really understood what Quark was—some kind of yogurt or a concoction made of whey, a byproduct of yogurt? Whatever it was, Nora disliked its sour tang.

Nora still sensed a reserve in Guy's manner and attempted to warm the atmosphere with a few stories about her interviews. Although Guy laughed in all the right places, the coolness abated only slightly. "OK, then. Let's get down to business," she said reluctantly to herself.

She began by describing her quirky relationship with Anna. When Nora and Mitch had last "house-sat" for Cary and Monika, the zucchinis were in full bloom in the back garden. She used them in salads and soups; she even tried a chocolate zucchini muffin recipe she found online but barely made a dent in Cary's supply. In desperation she gathered four of the biggest zucchinis in the patch and put them on the porch of the then-unknown neighbor, Anna. The next day, to her amazement, she found a plate of peaches on the pillar of the stone fence separating Cary's house from his neighbor's. Nora, in return, picked a quart of blackberries from the vines in the far corner of Cary's garden and placed these on the pillar in a bowl carefully balanced on the neighbor's plate. This exchange of homegrown produce continued for over a week until Nora worked up the courage to give her last contribution to Anna in person. She introduced herself in her grade school German, addressing Anna as Frau Herman, as did Cary and Monika.

"Nein, nein. Ich bin Anna, bitte." Later, when she told Cary and Monika about her first conversation with Anna, they were amazed. After three years as neighbors, they had not moved past a formal *Sie* relationship with their older neighbor. Nora suggested that their ages (both around sixty) created an instant bond between them.

Nora's story about Anna did not seem to convince Guy of her warmth and generosity but he agreed to serve as Nora's translator in the upcoming interview, bowing to Nora's supposed expertise in establishing a relationship with Anna that transcended language differences.

Anna's patio table in her sunroom was set with tea and small cakes on a beautiful flowered tray. Nora was beginning to feel a bit waterlogged from all the tea and coffee she'd already drunk that morning but knew that good manners dictated that she share a cup with Anna.

Anna had always lived in Lankwitz in the former East and was the oldest of the people Nora planned to interview. She was part of a group of East Germans in Berlin who protested against the Wall in the 1980s. Because of her political activity, Anna had constantly worried about being reported to the Stasi, East Germany's secret police.

When Anna and her husband were building their house in Lankwitz in the early seventies, she was so angry about the presence of guard dogs, manned watchtowers, and soldiers with machine guns near the building site that she marched resolutely up to one of the soldiers and said, "You know what this looks like? This looks like Buchenwald." This outburst sealed Anna's fate as a target for the Stasi.

Anna's house—where she still lives—is next to Cary and Monika's on Matthias-Pinkler Allee, one side of which was on the east side of the East/West border. The other side of the street was part of what was referred to as "no man's land"—a stretch about one hundred feet wide in front of the actual Wall. Everyone on Anna's street knew they were not allowed to cross to the other side of Matthias-Pinkler Allee where there were many apple trees.

Early in the eighties, a friend of Anna's fourteen-year-old daughter came to visit. This friend didn't know the unspoken rule against venturing across the street and unintentionally crossed it to pick an apple. She was quickly picked up by the *Polizei*, thrown into the back of a truck and taken to a holding facility in Postdam where her parents had to pick her up. After that, she was not allowed to attend school. It was also understood that she would not be able to enroll in university when she got older.

Anna's German was fast and heavily accented. Nora could see Guy struggling to capture her thoughts in his small black notebook. At Nora's urging, Anna remembered the day the Wall came down. Her best friend had been at a party listening to news reports on the radio. Anna's friend arrived in Anna's house and told her that people from the GDR were streaming through the checkpoints into the West. Anna's daughter immediately wanted to go into West Berlin, but Anna refused, insisting that she would go to work the next day and her daughter must go to school as usual. But when she got to work and her daughter arrived at school, there was no one at either place. So Anna dutifully went to the police and got permission for her and her daughter to go to the West. She showed Guy and Nora the document granting permission, carefully preserved in a plastic sleeve with the official stamp of the East German police.

A few days later, Anna's cousin from Leipzig came to visit but didn't know anything about the Wall coming down. So Anna announced, "We're going to the West." Their first destination was KaDeWe where Anna had often shopped before the Wall went up. Her friend had never been in Berlin's most elegant department store. Anna maintained that her cousin "nearly had a breakdown" because "she had never seen so many luxuries!"

The fall of the Wall had been both good and bad for Anna. Good, because the danger of doing or saying something that could get her reported to the Stasi was over. It was now possible for her to travel and "experience freedom." But the fall of the Wall was bad for her too, because when the Wall came down, a whole country of people instantly became unemployed, including Anna and her husband.

There were plenty of programs in unified Germany to retrain people from the former East for jobs in the new Germany. Anna received lots of training but, giddy with their newfound freedom to travel, she and her husband went to the United States for four weeks. When they came back, there was no job for Anna, partly because of her age (forties at that time). She had not been able to find full-time employment since, supporting herself with seasonal work like selling asparagus from a corner stand near her home.

Nora tried to decipher Anna's rapid-fire German but found herself distracted by the incredulous look on Guy's face. This was the first story about the Communist era in Germany he'd ever personally heard. He struggled to place it in some sort of context. His experience with German history was obviously colored by the Holocaust. From his vantage point, German history ended with the end of the war. Not so for Anna.

When they were back at Nora's flat, Guy related the details of Anna's monologue to Nora. Nora had understood a little of Anna's German, enough to verify that Guy's translation accurately captured the essence of Anna's experiences. Nora was anxious to find some way to repay Guy for his efforts. "Can I treat you to lunch?" she asked.

"No, but thank you. I have a meeting soon with my sister's solicitor. There is some question about the deed to her house." Guy rose to leave, extending his hand to Nora for a formal handshake. Instead, Nora placed a tentative hand softly on Guy's arm.

"Guy, I think I offended you the last time we met. I was not willing to hear *your* story. Please be patient with me and understand that I am certainly not thinking anything bad about you. It's just that I don't feel comfortable talking about the personal details of my life, and I don't want you to feel obligated to share the details of yours. Does that make sense to you?" Nora asked, hoping that this would clear the air between them.

Guy smiled at Nora—a genuine smile of relief. "Thank you for saying this. I do understand, but I am hoping that someday we can get to know each other better. I look forward to that."

Nora was doubtful about the possibility of that ever happening but nodded agreeably. They planned to meet later in the week at one of Nora's favorite Berlin haunts, Coffee Culture in Steglitz, a five-minute train ride from Zehlendorf.

*   *   *

Monika wanted to hear all the details of Nora's morning with Guy. Nora found she had few to provide but assured Monika that Guy seemed harmless. "He's really nice. He's a bit stiff and old-fashioned but nice. I like him. I think we'll become friends."

"Nora, Nora. Please be careful. You trust people too quickly."

"I know, Monika, but I'd rather be that way than go through life suspicious of everyone."

"Like me?"

"No," Nora laughed. "Not like you. I think you're just the right blend of cautious but interested," she assured Monika in the usual manner with which she warded off Monika's worries. Nora was afraid that Monika saw her as incapable of forming wise judgments about situations or people. "I'm not stupid," she said in an imaginary conversation with Monika. "I'm a grown woman with experience, and I can tell who and what I should watch out for. Guy is a good person. I don't care what he may or may not have done."

But for all her bravado, Nora had trouble stifling her curiosity. What *had* he done? There was an easy way to find out.

Making her excuses to Monika, Nora headed back to her flat. Later, she opened her laptop and settled in for an online exploration of Guy's past. She googled his name and found hundreds of entries. Most focused on one particular incident.

A newspaper article in the *International Global Review* dated July 10, 2009, gave her most of the details.

Trial of Belgian Architect Set for This Month

Prominent Belgian architect Guy Guzman will stand trial this month on charges of assault and battery for his alleged attack on Dr. Martin Zanger, an oncologist at Women's Christian Hospital in Brussels. Guzman was arrested on 27 September by a member of the Brussels gendarmerie attached to the Rue de la Loi 1 Guard station in Brussels. According to Zanger, Guzman threw him against a wall in the hospital when he informed Guzman of his wife's chances of surviving ovarian cancer. Guzman's wife Anais

Guzman passed away shortly after the incident. Zanger maintains that he sustained serious injury to his right arm and shoulder as a result of the 'attack.'

In an interview with the *Echo de la Bourse* newspaper in Brussels, Guzman did not deny his part in the incident. However, he defended his actions by suggesting that Zanger was at least partially responsible for his wife's declining condition. Guzman stated that he believed Zanger neglected to recommend treatment for his wife that could have prolonged her life. Guzman also suggested that Zanger's doctoring of his wife bordered on neglect. He asserted that this neglect was rooted in a deep-seated prejudice against Jews. Zanger had supposedly asked to be removed from the case when he discovered that Anais Guzman was one of the few surviving members of the Eisengruppe family who had dominated the European banking industry before WW2. Most members of the family died in the Bergen-Belsen concentration camp.

Dr. Zanger has consistently denied Guzman's accusations, asserting that Guzman overreacted to Zanger's pronouncement about Anais Guzman's condition. Zanger has accused Guzman of being a "hot head." He denies Guzman's accusations about his supposed anti-Semitism, suggesting that Guzman is "paranoid and given to histrionics."

As an architect, Guzman is well known in Europe for his avant guard use of natural materials in his building designs. Incorporating a pillar carved from a 15-foot spruce tree in his design of the main EU assembly hall in Strasbourg, France, earned him a reputation as the architect who best reflects the postmodern influences in the building designs of the 1980s.

Anticipating a large crowd for Guzman's upcoming trial, Judge Michel Vervouve, has relocated the trial to the largest courtroom in the Brussels judicial facility.

"So that's what it was all about," thought Nora. "But how did the trial turn out?" Despite another half hour of searching the Internet for the results of the trial, Nora found nothing. She believed Guy would willingly tell her what happened, but after reading the blurb from t*he Global Review*, she was even more determined not to ask. She realized that she wanted to think well of Guy, and the details of his trial might make that difficult. She wasn't burying her head in the sand, as Monika had implied, or adopting the "don't worry, be happy" attitude Mitch always accused her of. She assured herself that she was simply allowing her friendship with Guy to tell her all she needed to know about his past, criminal or otherwise.

*   *   *

Nora was still struggling with her ambivalence about Guy when she left the Steglitz train station and walked the two blocks to Coffee Culture. Guy was already there, sipping a cappuccino and reading a French-language newspaper. "Bonjour," he called out gaily, motioning her to his table in the corner. He stood to kiss Nora on both cheeks, French style. Nora was momentarily taken aback but reminded herself that she wasn't in the "no touching" zone of Midwestern America anymore.

Guy was full of questions about the interview with Anna. "Why was Anna's daughter's friend punished for just crossing a street?" "Why did Anna leave Germany for the US so soon after the Wall came down?" "Why can't Anna find a good job now that the economy is getting better in Germany?" "What happened to Anna's husband?"

Nora couldn't answer most of Guy's questions because Cary and Monika really knew very little about Anna except that she was a widow. They assumed her husband had been an important figure in the Communist party because her home was in an area where only the party elite lived in the old GDR. No one else could be trusted so close to a section of the Wall that could so easily be scaled.

"Guy, the reason for these interviews," Nora explained patiently, "is to see if people from East Germany are more satisfied with life in Germany after the Wall came down than people who lived in West Germany. The stories people tell me in these interviews are interesting but not necessarily revealing about the individuals themselves. I believe these stories are rapidly becoming something like folklore and may not really tell me how people feel about the unified Germany. Those thoughts tend to come later, after they've revisited their lives under the old systems in their stories. It's hard to explain, but it's a little like in the US when you ask people from New York about what they were doing when the Twin Towers were hit on 9/11. They have lots of stories about where they were when the first plane hit, as well as stories about friends and friends of friends who escaped or didn't. But these stories are not directly connected to New Yorkers' opinions on terrorism. Those come later."

"I don't understand the point of the interviews if it's not to learn more about the people."

"I think you'll have a better idea of what I'm hoping to learn after a few more interviews."

"So I'm to be your interpreter again?" said Guy with enthusiasm.

"Yes, if you're willing. I have an interview scheduled for this afternoon with my friend Mari. She speaks English fluently, but I think she might feel more comfortable speaking German. She lives way up in Pankow on the east side of Berlin north of Alexanderplatz, so it will take us a while to get there. Would you like to have lunch at my flat before we go up?"

"I have a better idea—one that will be less trouble for you. Why not come with me to my sister's house for lunch? She has a housekeeper that will make us a simple meal, and we can leave afterwards for Mari's. My sister's house is not far from here. It's in Dahlem. Do you know where that is?"

"Yes, I do, and I'd love to see your sister's house." Nora was excited, but not for the same reasons as Guy. She hoped that a visit to Lillet's house might shed some light on Guy's past without the sticky conversation with the burden of reciprocity Nora feared.

Guy told Nora a little more about his sister on the drive to Dahlem. "Lillet was a sweet little girl, but something changed when she got older. She sometimes became angry and violent for no reason. This horrible blackness of spirit would disappear as suddenly as it came, and we would have our sweet girl back again. We never knew when these moods would strike. Years later, I found out from my aunt that my sister was schizophrenic. I think perhaps my parents suspected something was wrong with Lillet even as a small child and were afraid she would be the first of all of us to be sent to a camp by the Nazis. The handicapped were, you know."

"But she must have been OK as an adult. How did she come to be in Berlin?"

"My aunt made sure that Lillet received excellent medical care when we returned to Belgium after the war. With medication, schizophrenics can lead normal lives. When Lillet was on her medication, she was one of the most charming women you can imagine. Luckily, she almost always took her medication, even though she said it made her feel slow and lazy. I used to laugh when she said this because I thought she was always lively."

"Like me with Anais, Lillet met her husband at university. They married and moved to Berlin after he graduated. He was a professor at Freie University in Berlin in the Psychology Department. Lillet didn't really have a career, but she helped Rolf with many of his research projects. Here we are." Guy motioned toward an imposing Baroque villa sided in shades of gray and rimmed with cream-colored embellishments around its roofline. Its architecture reminded Nora of the much-loved Wedgewood china she inherited from her mother. The house's many tall windows looked out over a street canopied by beautiful old elm trees.

"Wow!" breathed Nora. "It's incredible!"

"Thank you. Lillet loved it. It was really too big for her after Rolf died, but she was determined to keep it in the family. I never understood how she planned to make this happen since she didn't have children."

Parking his Lupo on the street in front of the house, Guy led Nora through a spacious foyer into what appeared to be a library.

The house's historic exterior belied an interior that was all modern sleekness—glass, chrome, and silk upholstery. Low-slung chairs were covered in pale blue brocade that matched the color of the Berlin sky on a rare sunny winter day. A mahogany grand piano in the corner contrasted sharply with the lightness of the room and its furnishings.

Seeing Nora eye the piano, he asked, "Do you play?"

"No. My mother did, though. She would have loved this piano," Nora said softly as she stroked the piano's satiny finish.

"Was your mother a musician?"

"No, she was just a housewife, but she studied music in college. I think if she hadn't met my father, she might have pursued a career in music. But women in America didn't normally do that sort of thing in the 1950s. After the war, they were mostly interested in making a nice home for the returning veterans."

"That was true in Europe too. Please, sit down. I will tell Helena there will be two for lunch."

Nora's eyes scanned the large room, looking for family photos. She found only one—a small picture on a bookshelf of two children with an older woman. On closer inspection, one of the children was actually a teenager, but the guileless look on both the boy's and the girl's faces suggested that they shared a childlike trust in the woman who stood between them.

"That is my sister and I with my Aunt Aimee," said Guy as he stepped into the library. "That photograph was taken shortly after we returned from Sweden at the end of the war. We barely knew my aunt then but we had no one else to count on to take good care of us. And as I told you before, she did."

"Didn't your sister have any other pictures of your family— your mother or father?"

"No, I'm afraid not. When the Nazis came to take away the Jews, people had little time to gather photos or other family mementos. When they arrived at the camps, the Nazis took anything of value the Jews managed to sneak out of their homes," Guy explained. "I would give everything I own for just one picture of my parents. I barely remember them. My mother had red hair, though. Sometimes I dream about rooms full of women with red hair and me searching the room for my mother among all the women. I've had that dream for as long as I can remember."

Nora thought about her own vivid dreams about her parents and quickly changed the subject. "Let me tell you about Mari before we go to meet her. Mari is in her early thirties. I met her through my brother. They are both in the choir at my brother's church. Mari sings like an angel. It's funny, though. Her father was a pastor of a Lutheran church in East Germany but she seems to have no interest in attending Lutheran services. She's not Catholic, but she always goes to a Catholic church."

"Perhaps she wanted to make a break with her past for some reason," Guy suggested.

"Maybe. I really don't know but I'll think you'll like her. She's very charming and," added Nora, "she has red hair."

"Then I'm sure I'll like her."

A large woman with broad hips and a blond braid coiled around her head stomped into the room. "I have lunch all ready for you, Herr Guzman. Would you like to eat in here or in the dining room?"

"*Dankeschon*, Helena. I think we'll eat in here."

"Oh gosh, look at the time," Nora said anxiously, glancing at her watch. "We'll have to eat quickly. I told Mari we'd meet her by two, and it's almost one now."

Guy and Nora managed to gulp down their lunch of a simple stew served with thick slices of German bread. "Perhaps afterwards we could stop at my favorite place for *Apfel Streudel*. My treat," Nora said as she finished the last drop of her *Apfel Shorle*, a mixture of apple juice and sparkling water.

"What does 'my treat' mean?"

"I'll explain later. We really must go now."

*   *   *

Mari freely admitted that some might see her as a "'drama queen.'" She picked up this expression when she lived in the US

70

for a few months with an American friend. At thirty-three, Mari looked back on her childhood in the GDR with mixed feelings. More than anyone else Nora interviewed, Mari was deeply disillusioned about the aftermath of the fall of the Wall. She believed the 'new Germany' should have risen phoenix-like from the ashes of both the East *and* the West. This, she felt, was far from what actually happened.

Mari spent her early childhood in a small village in East Germany where her father was the pastor of the town's Lutheran church. When she was eight years old, her family moved to Pankow in the northeastern corner of what was then East Berlin.

The clergy were not well thought of in Communist East Germany. Mari was often bullied by her new classmates who were the children of Communist-party bigwigs and possibly—although it was never openly stated—informers employed by the Stasi.

Mari's mother and father had both been politically active. Her mother distributed pamphlets all over the Eastern side of Berlin condemning the Wall. "Whenever my mother left on a train to distribute these flyers, we were never certain when—and if—she'd return," Mari told Nora and Guy.

"My father was part of a group of clergy who participated in 'Monday prayers.' These were peaceful vigils in several cities in East Germany where candles were lit and prayers offered for the end of the autocratic government of the GDR.

"The day the Wall came down, my father piled us in our little Trabi and drove across the border to visit one of his old colleagues." Mari remembered how they approached the house in an upscale neighborhood in West Berlin and were mystified that the ultramodern structure of glass and steel was where people actually lived. "When we went inside, the host family surprised us with a big German breakfast. We had never seen so many pastries and sausages! There were even teddy bear-shaped sausages for the children! My brother and sister and I were awestruck by all the toys in the children's bedrooms," Mari added.

Explaining her mixed feelings about the new unified Germany, Mari maintained, "It's great that the freedom my parents fought for was actually achieved, but I wonder, was this freedom just to give us more kinds of yogurt in the supermarket?" Surely her parents' efforts were wasted if the biggest impact of reunification was introducing Western-style consumerism to East Germans.

Rubbing her temples in frustration, Mari maintained that it is politically incorrect to say anything good about the old GDR. "But," she said softly, "it really wasn't all bad. People pulled together in the GDR when someone was in need. When a person required something new, the word we used in the GDR for purchasing actually translates into English as 'organizing' rather than 'buying' because we usually got a new coat or a piece of furniture by bartering." This organizational process often included more than one or two transactions. Someone might trade A for B, and the new owner of B might trade it for C, who might then trade the needed item with A for something else again.

Walking Nora and Guy to her gray apartment building's front door, Mari said with impassioned certainty, "Erasing a country and a culture was hurtful. Reunification should have occurred more slowly and been more a meeting of two equal countries." The new Germany, she maintained, should have been a joint creation of the East and West, not simply the absorption of East Germany into the West.

"Wow," Nora exclaimed. "I never heard Mari talk like that before. We usually talk about her music or her career as a social worker, but never about politics."

"But you asked her to talk about this. Did you want her to refuse you? I think you should accept what she said as a gift, something precious given to you because she trusts you to use it wisely," said Guy.

"I never thought of it like that. You know, Guy, you wouldn't have had to come with me. Mari's English is almost perfect, so I really didn't need you to interpret. I don't know why I thought I needed you with me."

"Just consider it another gift," Guy said amiably.

"I didn't give much thought to this project before I began. It was mainly a way to justify getting out of the US. But having you with me, listening to these stories alongside you, makes me see that what I'm doing could be important."

"Then perhaps I *am* giving you a gift! Shall we celebrate all this gift-giving with a glass of sekt or perhaps a glass of fine Belgian beer?"

"Maybe next time. I think I want to go home and think about all this. Can I call you soon to set up another interview?"

"Of course," said Guy, obviously disappointed.

They arrived back at Nora's flat. She was deep in thought as she climbed the stairs and let herself into her apartment. Something was happening to her. She didn't know what and, more importantly, she didn't know whether it was good or bad. What she did know is that it felt dangerous.

Chapter 9

"You like Guy and you're getting closer to him," Monika said as she and Nora worked companionably in Monika's kitchen, Nora sautéing mushrooms and Monika slicing onions.

"Of course I like him, but we're not close. We're more like, uh . . . research buddies."

"Nora, there is no such thing as 'research buddies' in Germany."

"But he's Belgian, remember?"

"I doubt they have such a thing in Belgium either."

"Maybe not, but what they do have is the world's greatest chocolate!" proclaimed Cary as he caught the tail end of the conversation.

"That's not what we were talking about!" Monika flicked Cary with the nearest dish towel. "I was telling Nora that I think she and Guy might be getting close."

"Is that true, Nora?" Cary asked, suddenly very serious.

"I really don't think so, but maybe I should slow things down a bit. I won't call him for the next interview. I think I'll let a week or so pass and then call him."

"I'm still worried about what he's hiding," said Monika. Her tears flowed as she sliced a last bit of onion and spooned the onions into the frying pan with the mushrooms.

"Don't worry so much. I googled him and found out most of what happened to him. I really don't want to know anything more."

"What are you afraid you'll find out?" asked Cary.

"I'm not afraid, and I wish you'd stop saying things like that. You two accuse me of being foolhardy and then, in the next breath, suggest that I'm standoffish or something. Anyway, I think I'll head on home. I have some work to do," Nora said as she tramped out of the kitchen, grabbing her coat from a rack near the front entrance. "See you later."

"I think we hurt her feelings, Cary," said Monika, regretting her part in what Nora had obviously seen as a confrontation.

"Monika, Nora needs her feelings hurt. She always does this. I think of it as her 'push me—pull you' maneuver. She gets a little close to someone, then pulls back. She can repeat this pattern over and over if she isn't called on it. I think that's the main reason she and Mitch fought so much. He never let her get away with that, and she couldn't forgive him for trying to force her to confront her demons."

"But what are these 'demons'?"

"I think they're her feelings about our parents dying so suddenly. She was really close to my father in particular. She was his 'best girl.' He always told her how special she was. I think she hasn't forgiven him for leaving her."

"But she had so much otherwise. She had Mitch and the boys and a wonderful career and"—Monika's eyes shone as she stroked Cary's back—"a wonderful brother too."

"But none of us seemed to be able to fill the hole my father left in her life. I think she resented Mitch for even trying."

"This is all so confusing to me. Let's eat. *Ich bin sehr hungrig!*"

"I'm hungry too, and now that Nora's not eating dinner here, all the more for us!"

*   *   *

Nora walked slowly back to her flat. Whenever something troubled her, she thought of a lecture she once heard by a man who suffered from Tourette's syndrome. He described his urge to shout out "damn" or "shit" as a persistent "internal itch" that couldn't be scratched. When something bothered her, Nora thought of it as her own private "inside itch." Until she could scratch it, she would never find relief. But scratching it could cause a sore spot to become even more irritated. Better to leave it alone and try to distract herself with something pleasant.

Nora knew in her heart that this was a childish way to deal with grief. She'd experienced three too many deaths in her lifetime, but instead of her feelings of loss diminishing to an intermittent drizzle, her grief seemed to grow over the years to tsunami proportions. She was like one of the three little pigs, throwing her weight against a fragile door that would soon be demolished by the big bad wolf.

But she put aside her metaphors and similes for the lingering sadness and tried to settle into a routine to keep herself busy. She began most days with breakfast in the café below her flat with what Nora had come to think of as the "Leben-ers." The men in the group grudgingly included her in their conversations despite their scorn for her grade-school German. They always left a few minutes before Katya and Paula. That left Nora to "dish the dirt" with the two young women. When she and her old friend Cele had commuted to Minton College together, they called their commute "dish time." Nora hadn't heard much from Cele since arriving in Germany. This didn't surprise her. Cele would be in the thick of a new semester with a whole new crowd of history students to introduce to the Civil War.

All Katya and Paula could talk about was a concert they planned to attend Friday evening after work. The featured band was famous for its unlikely combination of Celtic-techno. For three mornings in a row, they begged Nora to come with them. Although she didn't say it, she thought it sounded horrible; but Katya and Paula were so persistent, she was seriously considering going with them.

In the afternoons, Nora visited her favorite haunts— Zehlendorf's tiny public library as well as Zehlendorf's much larger

Starbucks, Café Culture or the Hugen Dubel café in Steglitz. When she felt especially ambitious, she made a pilgrimage to the Hugen Dubel on the Ku-Damm. Unfortunately she could only access the Internet at some of her hangouts. Unlike in the US, Germany didn't seem to have many free Wi-Fi spots. Although the public library offered Wi-Fi, patrons were charged one euro an hour for a terribly slow connection. Somehow Nora managed to check her e-mail almost every day, savoring messages from her sons. Michael's were always filled with his views on politics, outrageous jokes, and silly photos of himself taken with his phone camera. Trevor's were short and businesslike—"How are you? I'm fine. Not much new here. Trev."

Trevor hated what he thought of as showy displays of affection. Even as a little boy of three and four, he refused to allow her to hold his hand when they crossed a busy street. When he started school, she resorted to bribing him with M&M's for kisses. Nora understood Trevor's standoffishness because she believed it disguised a softer side. If she hadn't known this before she certainly saw it when Trevor was around twenty.

Trevor's best friend died when they were both sophomores in college. At Andy's funeral, Nora couldn't help crying when she saw all the strong young men with tears streaming down their faces. Trevor slipped his arm around his mother's shoulders. It remained there throughout the long funeral service. Nora never forgot this effort to console her. Although they didn't talk about it, Nora was convinced that the tears she cried were those he himself shed beneath his reserved exterior.

Although Trevor had always consulted Mitch on money matters he clearly saw his mother as the family expert on relationships, something for which he himself had little appreciation. When a former girlfriend trashed Trevor's apartment after he asked her for a few weeks' "space" to reacclimate to the US after a semester in Thailand, it was to his mother that Trevor turned to help him understand what he saw as a totally irrational act. "We agreed to be friends," he moaned to Nora.

"You may have agreed to that, but she obviously felt differently," Nora said dryly. The truth was that she too was dumbfounded by the ex-girlfriend's inexplicable behavior.

*   *   *

Nora managed to keep busy most of the time in Berlin, but the late afternoon/early evening hours often seemed to drag on endlessly. As daylight waned, Nora had taken to riding the S-Bahn trains to the end of their lines. When she needed a small, effortless adventure she went to Frohnau, in the far north of Berlin. It was a long train ride from where Nora lived—nearly an hour on the S-1 line. First, the train rattled through the tree-lined neighborhoods of Lichterfelde-West, Botanischer Garten, and Friedenau. Then things took on a rougher look in Schoneberg, Yorckstrasse, and in the Anhalter Bahnhof. Next, the train hit tourist central Berlin where confused travelers stumbled off the train to be replaced by harried Berliners bound for the northern suburbs. Nora, the non-resident/non-tourist, was one of the few passengers remaining from the group that first boarded the S-1 in Zehlendorf.

The train rumbled north through Potsdamer Platz, Unter den Linden, and Friedrich Strasse. Nordbahnhof and Humboldthain were next. Nora found these areas gritty and forbidding. ("Don't make the mistake of getting off here, innocent American lady," they warned her.) On to Wittenau, Waidmannslust, and finally, Frohnau. The platform at Frohnau foretold the *Gemütlichkeit* (warm coziness) of the small tree-lined community. Its faded green wooden benches with high carved sides cradled their infrequent passengers while they waited for the next train.

Frohnau was well off the beaten path for most visitors to Berlin. Nora's presence in its tiny shops and bistros appeared to be unusual. When she visited an antique shop there one day, the owner ceremoniously presented her with a single white rose from a vase of roses prominently displayed on a carved bureau. There didn't seem to be anything unusual going on in the shop (a big blow-out sale?). Nora suspected that a lone American woman who "oohed and ahhed" over German antiques was probably the only thing out of the ordinary for the shopkeeper that day.

Nora made her treks to Frohnau when she felt overwhelmed with the sheer *work* of life in Berlin. Walking or cycling (yes, she had a bicycle which she rode sporadically) to the nearest train station or navigating buses, stores, and restaurants with her limited German—this all took energy. "I'm actually getting pretty good at it," she thought to herself, but it all demanded so much from her. Sometimes riding the train to Frohnau with the multiple personalities of Berlin's streets rushing past her window was all she could muster in the way of a diversion. Once she got to Frohnau, there really wasn't a lot to keep her there—a few boutiques, a wonderful tea shop, and her favorite Italian restaurant. Occasionally, she turned around and rode home almost immediately. But even a glimpse of Frohnau with its velvety lawns and stately stucco villas refreshed her soul and fortified her for more strenuous adventures in Berlin life.

But loneliness was never more than a hair's breath away. Cary was gone for several weeks chaperoning his school's eighth-grade ski trip in Austria. ("Wow, what a life," Nora thought to herself.) Monika was off on another business trip and not due home until Friday. Nora thought about contacting some of the German friends she'd met through Connections, the English-language club in Berlin of which Cary was currently president. But they all worked during the day, and she was wary of riding the trains after dark to meet them for dinner or drinks.

So she "jammied up" (as Mitch referred to her habit of slipping on her pajamas as soon as the sun set) and settled in for long evenings of German television. Savoring her daily glass of prosecco, she worked crosswords puzzles and glanced at the TV screen whenever she heard a word or phrase she understood. Her mind often drifted to Guy.

Friday morning her cell phone rang just as she was packing up her laptop for a trip to the Zehlendorf library.

"Nora. This is Guy."

Nora gulped. What could she say? She wanted to see him, but she was afraid of getting entangled in his life. "Hello, Guy, how are you?"

"I am well, but I wanted you to know that I'm leaving Berlin for a week or so. I need to return to Belgium to sell my flat there. I've decided to stay in Berlin for a while. Settling my sister's estate is taking longer than I thought it would." He paused for several seconds. "I wondered if you'd care to join me for a short trip to Brussels?"

Almost every instinct in her told her to say no, but Nora found herself agreeing. It was better than sitting around waiting for Cary and Monika to return, she reasoned.

"Will we drive or take a train?" Nora asked.

"I'd like to drive if it's all right with you. It's a long drive—almost eight hours, but the countryside is very interesting. I think you might enjoy it."

"Eight hours is nothing in the US. My husband and I used to drive more than that to visit friends in Washington. When will we leave?"

"Saturday morning early—around nine o'clock?"

"I'll be ready."

Saturday was only a few days away, but Nora still had the Friday-night concert to endure. She met Katya and Paula in Das Süße Leben for a quick snack. Then they were off. They took a bus to Zehlendorf, then a train to a stop near Freie University, followed by another bus to the concert site. The concert was in an old warehouse not far from the campus. Nora could hear the steady beat from a quarter mile away—*thup . . . thup-thup, thup . . . thup-thup.*

"I'm too old for this," she said to herself, grimacing as the relentless beat grew louder and louder. A twentysomething crowd was packed shoulder to shoulder in the dank warehouse.

"It's great, isn't it?" Katya's eyes shone as she melted into the crowd, Paula following close behind.

"How will I ever get through this?" Nora thought. "I've got a headache already." She had a long evening ahead. The band on the makeshift stage was only a warm-up for the main event: Flinging Mary.

Katya and Paula seemed to know nearly everyone in audience. They called out greetings in German and English as they made their way to an empty spot on the floor near a huge amplifier.

"Mary is up next," shouted Paula. As soon as she said it, the warm-up band finished their last song with a flourish. For one blissful second, silence ensued. Then eight men ran onto the stage, each heavily pierced and tattooed, wearing dirty kilts and torn T-shirts. The applause was deafening.

Flinging Mary's array of instruments included the standard keyboard and electric guitars with the addition of an accordion, a flute, and a small Irish drum called a "bodhrán." Nora had read about this Celtic instrument with a goatskin tacked to one side of its circular frame. The other side was open-ended for a hand to rest against the inside of the drumhead to control its pitch and timbre.

When the band started playing, it was almost as if the entire crowd of five or six hundred people were jumping in sync on the world's largest trampoline—up, down, up, down, up, down. Nora felt her heart stop, then restart, aligning itself with the relentless beat. She was bombarded by sound—not just of the music, but of the endless screaming. "Kind of like being in a burning building, but not as scary," she thought to herself. She decided the only way she could tolerate the experience was to try to view it through the unbiased eye of a researcher.

Katya and Paula were transfixed. Their sweet young faces were lifted like sunflowers toward the reflective light of five strobes. They gave no thought to Nora and any possible discomfort she might be experiencing. They assumed she felt as they did—totally engulfed in the driving beat of Flinging Mary.

The strong, sweet smell of marijuana filled the air, but Nora saw no joints being passed. "There must be some corner of the room that's the officially designated smoking spot." She decided to try to find it.

She told Katya that she was going to wander a bit, although "wander" was a misnomer. "Sidle" was a better description of the easing and pushing movement necessary for moving through the enormous crowd. Not surprisingly, the drug corner was strategically located in front of the bathrooms. One needed to run the gauntlet of a dense blue haze to use the facilities. Someone shoved a joint into Nora's hand, and she took a tentative toke. "Yup, that's kind of how I remember it." She returned the joint to its owner and continued to the women's toilet.

It was not silent in the bathroom, but still, the decibel level was at least 25 percent lower. "Whew." She breathed a sigh of relief, vowing to stay in the bathroom as long as she could. Thirty minutes later, she had exhausted the entertainment value of the four-stall restroom and reluctantly eased her way back into the crowd to find Katya and Paula. They were now writhing frenetically in front of the stage.

"I think I'm going to go now," Nora told Katya.

Paula straightened up and exchanged looks with Katya. "We made a bet on how long you would be able to stand it. I bet two hours, and Katya said one."

"Neither of you won. It's been one and a half hours. But thank you for inviting me. It's been very interesting, but I think my head will explode if I stay much longer." Nora waved good-bye to Katya and Paula and eased her way to the exit. Once outside, the night air smelled fresh and clean, and the sudden freedom to move prompted a moonlit walk.

"I think I'll skip the bus and just walk to the train station. I don't think the station is that far." She argued with her cautious self that walking alone at night was much safer in Berlin than in the average big city in the US. The crime rate in Berlin *was* much lower than in Chicago, for instance.

Just as she was mentally reviewing comparative crime statistics, a huge form emerged from the shadows. "*Hey, haben Sie etwas Kleingeld, Madam?*" said the form, which turned out to be a bald man in his early thirties accompanied by a huge rottweiler with a studded collar and choke chain.

"Here," Nora said as she thrust a one-euro coin into a grubby hand. She turned and ran back to the bus stop. "*Danke sehr, gnadige*

Frau!" (gracious lady) called the form as his dog launched a series of deep-throated barks. Nora felt a touch of guilt at the surprisingly polite thank-you. "You're not in Chicago anymore, Dorothy," she thought as she fashioned a wry half-smile.

The bus to the station came just as Nora approached the stop. There were at least fifteen passengers on the bus, all headed for the station. The train arrived almost as soon as Nora got to the platform. Back in Lankwitz, her courage returned and she walked the ten blocks back to her flat. Her head was still pounding but she knew she would sleep deeply. "No dreams tonight," she assured herself. And she was right.

Chapter 10

Nora woke with her head still pounding. It took her several minutes to recognize that the pounding was coming from her front door. Guy! Throwing off her duvet, she bolted from bed. "I'm so sorry, Guy," she said as she threw open her door.

He glanced disapprovingly at her oversized cotton T-shirt. "Did I come too early? It's almost nine."

"No, no. You're right on time. It's just that I was out late last night at a concert with some friends and forgot to set my alarm when I got back home. I'm so sorry," she said again. "I'll just grab some things and we can go." Luckily, she had packed the day before, so she needed only to take a quick shower. She skipped her usual elaborate makeup routine and dressed simply in cotton pants and a white linen shirt.

"All set. Are you ready?" she asked in a tone that suggested that it was Guy who might not be ready rather than her.

"Have you had breakfast?" Guy asked.

"No, but we can grab something downstairs."

Das Süße Leben had just opened, but the Saturday breakfast crowd proved to be larger than its weekday crowd. Guy and Nora waited in line for croissants and coffee. Several people stared at

Nora and Guy. "Did I forget a shoe or something? People are staring at us."

"I think they are staring at me, Nora. Just ignore them. I always do."

Nora puzzled over this but decided it was too early and she was still too sleepy to pursue it. They ordered their breakfast *mitnahmen* (to go)—something new in Germany—and headed to the Lupo, which was parked a half-block away. Guy had placed a small cardboard clock on his dashboard, set for twenty minutes after nine.

"What's this?" Nora asked as she grabbed the piece of cardboard and settled into her seat.

"We are on the honor system for parking here," Guy explained. "One moves the clock hands to the time you plan to return to the car, and if you stay longer than that, you may get a parking ticket."

"Ingenious," Nora breathed. German efficiency at work again.

Guy aimed the little Lupo toward the westbound autobahn out of the city. "Do you mind if I read?" Nora asked as she pulled her IPod out of her purse.

"What do you have there?" Guy glanced at the small device.

"This is an IPod. I have many books on it. My son loaded them for me before I left the US. That way, I always have lots to read without packing too many books in my suitcase. Books weigh so much and now the airlines are charging for checked bags, so I really have to watch how much I pack."

"So you have a son."

"Two, actually. Michael is my oldest. He's thirty-five, and Trevor is twenty-nine. Do you have any children?"

"No. Sadly, my wife was unable to get pregnant. But we had many friends with children. We were always taking care of other people's children. Anais was a great favorite with them. We were Uncle Guy and Aunt Anais to half of Liege!"

"How did you happen to end up in Brussels?"

"I moved there after Anais died. Our house in Liege seemed so big and empty with her gone. I also had many clients in Brussels, so it was more practical for me to move there and buy a flat. I sold our house in Liege to a friend, so I know it is well taken care of. Anais would have wanted that."

"Why do you want to sell your flat now?" Nora suspected she was being a little nosey, but that didn't stop her.

"I like Berlin even though it has a bad past for someone who is Jewish, but I sometimes think that makes it the best time to live in Berlin. There is much remorse over the Holocaust among the younger people, so older Germans of my age keep their mouths shut if they disagree. It's a good arrangement. Besides, I have a new friend in Berlin I'd like to know better," he said, looking pointedly at Nora.

She ducked her head and pretended to be engrossed in her IPod book.

Nora read for several hours until Guy announced, "Time for lunch."

He sounded so much like Mitch at that moment that Nora had to laugh. Mitch had always insisted on driving straight through to every destination—no matter how far—with only one stop per trip. He had always ceremoniously announced a stop in the same way: "Time for lunch." It didn't matter what time of day it was. "Lunch" always signified food, bathroom, gas, and stretching one's legs—the all-purpose respite. Nora sensed Guy would be more flexible.

They pulled off the autobahn at the Leopoldschohe exit and drove up to a small country inn. It was typical of the timberframe houses in Germany with rough-hewn slats bisecting colorful walls that met at the highest point of a steeply peaked roof. This one was a faded rose with what looked like watercolors lifted from a book of German fairy tales painted on panels on either side of the doors and windows. There was "Hansel and Gretel" (*Hänsel und Gretel*), "Cinderella" (*Aschenputtel*), and "Rapunzel" on the front; "The Fisherman and His Wife" (*Von dem Fischer und seiner Frau*) and "Rumpelstiltskin" (*Rumpelstilzchen*) were painted on the sides of the building.

"This inn is where I had my first German meal," said Guy. "It wasn't terribly good, but the atmosphere was enchanting. It's probably the same now. Shall we see?"

"Oh yeah." There was no question that Nora was ready to explore the inside of the inn.

The inn's interior proved to be as charming as its exterior but as Guy predicted, the food was not memorable—heavy stews drowning in greasy sauces served in earthenware crocks. But Nora's dessert was wonderful. Classic *Apfel Struedel* wrapped in light flakey pastry, topped with a sweet vanilla sauce and a dollop of dense German *Sahne*, the rich whipped crème so thick it almost passed for mousse.

"Mmmm . . ." she sighed, savoring the last bite. "Now I'm ready for a nap."

As they pulled away from the inn, Nora's eyelids drooped. The big meal and the previous night's encounter with the world of punk both took their toll. When she woke, Guy was pulling into an underground parking garage. "Where are we?" she asked.

"We are here in Brussels. My flat is around the corner."

Guy's flat was in the heart of Brussels. It was a short walk from the Grand-Place, Brussel's huge town square with its patchwork of a dozen architecturally diverse buildings originally created to house the guilds of the city's tradesmen. The Grand-Place is considered one of the most beautiful squares in Europe, home now to Godiva Chocolate and several luxurious hotels.

An old-fashioned elevator with ornate grillwork took Nora and Guy to the top floor of a building at least two hundred years old. Unlocking his front door, Guy motioned Nora into a narrow corridor that fanned out into a sitting room with floor-to-ceiling windows overlooking a park. The furniture was old and worn but of excellent quality. The wooden pieces bore the warm patina of age. An oriental rug of rich blues and deep greens was the only thing in the room that looked to be less than fifty years old.

Guy showed Nora to the guest bedroom, and they agreed to meet in an hour for an early dinner. Nora stretched out on a canopied bed covered with a silk duvet and promptly fell asleep again. She woke to find shadows creeping across the room. She jumped up and bounded into the living room where Guy sat at a small writing desk.

"Why didn't you wake me? It must be almost eight!"

"I tried but you were sleeping so soundly. I did not want to disturb you. Are you hungry for dinner now?"

"Guy, can we go to the Grand-Place and eat? I read that one can get the best Belgian waffles in the Grand-Place."

Guy wrinkled his nose at the allure of Belgian waffles for American tourists. "All right. Just this once."

They walked the short block to the Grand-Place and enjoyed warm Belgian waffles and french fries served the Belgian way with lots of mayonnaise. After a leisurely stroll around the square followed by a glass of Belgian beer, they headed back to Guy's flat.

Over the next few days, Guy was busy consulting with his attorney and finding a listing agent for his flat. He also found time to sort through the few mementos of his childhood in Belgium with his sister and his Aunt Aimee.

Nora occupied her days exploring Brussels. She was taken with the quirky Belgian humor encapsulated in *Manneken Pis*, the statue of a little boy peeing irreverently into a beautiful cascade of flowers. She also particularly enjoyed the Atomium. Built for the 1958 World Fair, the Atomium represents a molecule's nine atoms, magnified 165 billion times. Something of a symbol of the city, it provides a panoramic view of Brussels and its surroundings. The nine spheres that make up the "atom" are linked by escalators. She especially loved the small things about Brussels like the patches of lavender planted in lush clumps on many of the traffic islands in the middle of busy intersections. The scent of lavender wafted over pedestrians while they waited patiently for the WALK/DON'T WALK sign to change.

The highlight of her stay in Brussels, however, was a visit to a plenary session in the European Union Headquarters. She wasn't sure, but she thought the room where the session was held was the room Guy had designed. On the day of her visit, there was a small group of EU members debating the acceptance of Turkey into the EU. The circular debating chamber had two levels, a ground level for EU members with an overhead tier for their army of interpreters. No decisions were made the day Nora visited. Turkey retained its "most favored nation" status, but EU membership remained elusive. Nora was reminded of the many Turks in Berlin who left their mark on the city with their spicy contributions to the bland German diet.

In the evenings, Guy and Nora dined at several of the finest restaurants in Brussels. Their conversations were mostly limited to food and travel. Guy shared a few stories about his sister and her husband in the hopes of drawing similar stories from Nora, but she remained "tight-lipped," as her brother Cary would have described it.

On their last night in Brussels, Guy took Nora to his favorite Italian restaurant, Castella Banfi, which occupies an eighteenth-century town house decorated in an Art Nouveau design. Black leather banquettes strategically placed between marble columns contrast sharply with snowy white linen and gilt-framed mirrors. Nora scanned the eight-page menu looking for her favorite pasta dish. She was perplexed. All the entrees were in Italian.

"Shall I order for you, Nora?"

"Yes. That would be great." She breathed a sigh of relief and settled into the soft leather of the banquette. "Did you take care of your business today, Guy?"

"No, I'm afraid not. There is a problem with the building itself. It seems there was an agreement among the tenants that no one could sell until all of the necessary building repairs were completed. The building was in need of new roof and there was talk of adding additional insulation. The new roof was installed last month, but it is not clear whether the insulation was formally incorporated into the tenant agreement or whether it was just discussed by some of the tenants. So I will need to stay a few more days to resolve this before the sale can be finalized. Are you willing to stay two or three more days?"

"Of course. There is still more for me to explore in Brussels. Besides, there are at least five more chocolate shops I need to visit. Did you know that paprika can be added to chocolate? It gives it a really unusual 'zip.'"

"Nora, you amaze me. I would never describe chocolate as having 'zip.' Chocolate is serious business in Brussels, very competitive. It's become quite the trend to add unusual ingredients to one's chocolate recipe to make it distinct from everyone else's."

They chatted amiably about chocolate for a while. Guy had many acquaintances in Brussels who owned and operated family chocolate businesses. Then their conversation moved on to the Castella Banfi's extensive wine list.

"I like many of the sparkling white wines in Europe, but what I really like here in Belgium is the Lambic beer, especially the strawberry-flavored one," confessed Nora. "It's kind of like a Kir Royale, but with strawberry instead of the usual black currant flavor. Mmmm."

*   *   *

"You! How dare you show your face here?" a woman shrieked at Guy from across the crowded room at Castella Banfi. "You arrogant bastard! It's not enough that you destroyed his life but you must flaunt it as well!"

A short red-faced blonde strode across the room and planted her small feet firmly in front of Guy. From a distance, she looked to be around forty, but at closer view, Nora could see that extensive cosmetic surgery had not extended to a crepey neck common among women in their early sixties.

"Mara, please, I had nothing to do with destroying his life. He did that all on his own."

"How dare you? What you put him through caused his heart attack. You know that and I know that, and don't try to deny it."

"I *do* deny it. I did no such thing. I am sorry for what happened to your husband. Perhaps we can discuss this in private at another time."

Heads were turning, curious to catch Guy's reactions to the small woman's accusations.

"No you don't," Mara shrieked again. "We will discuss it now. I won't be put off!"

Guy stood. "Nora, I think we must leave. We will come back another time."

Nora slipped on her light cotton sweater. She stood shoulder to shoulder with Guy. "I don't know what happened to your husband, and frankly, I don't care," she said in a calm voice that belied her embarrassment. "But Guy would never deliberately hurt anyone without provocation." Nora was determined to present a united front with Guy before this woman who accused him so viciously.

With a firm hand Guy steered Nora past the irate woman and the small crowd that had gathered around her. "You will see! He will hurt you too. He cannot do otherwise!" Mara screamed at Nora's retreating figure.

"Nora, I am so sorry. I thought that was all over, but I now think it may never be over for Mara," Guy explained when they were safely outside the restaurant. Mara had followed main dining room to rejoin her table of astonished friends.

"Guy, you have nothing to apologize for. Let's just forget it. I'm not very hungry now, but I am a bit tired. I think I'd just like to go back to the flat."

They walked in silence back to Guy's flat. After sharing a quick snack with Guy, Nora retired to her room.

*   *   *

Nora saw it in the distance. The lights were blinding. She heard a high-pitched whine that could only be a human scream. Crimson waves rolled over her field of vision. Something was coming at her. She threw up her arms to protect her face. She couldn't stop it. It was approaching so fast—a blur punctuated by flashes of light. What was it, and why didn't Mitch try to stop it? She felt him by her side but knew he'd do nothing. She grabbed for him, but he slipped out of her grasp. Where was he going?

"Don't leave me," she sobbed and flung herself into waiting arms. Panting roughly, she was drenched in sweat.

Guy tightened his hold. "Nora, Nora. You are safe. I won't leave you." He stroked her back gently.

Nora woke. She blinked rapidly. "Oh, Guy! I'm so sorry! Did I wake you?" She pulled away and drew her knees up to her chest.

Ever the little girl, thought Guy. "Don't worry. That's not important. Something was obviously distressing you very much. Can you tell me about it? It might make you feel better."

"It was nothing. Just the same old dream I've had for many years."

"Nora, it did not seem like nothing. Are you sure it wouldn't help to talk about it?"

"No, but thank you, Guy. I appreciate the offer, but I think some things are better left alone."

"We can talk about it in the morning if you change your mind."

"I won't. And, Guy, I think I'll go back to Berlin tomorrow. I'll just take a train. I know you have more business here, but I'm ready to go back."

"As you like," Guy said stiffly. "I will drive you to the train station in the morning."

"Please don't bother. I'll take a taxi," Nora said resolutely and turned over on her side, pretending to drift off to sleep.

Nora had plenty of time to think about Mara's confrontation in the restaurant as well as Guy's reaction to her nightmare on the long train ride to Berlin. She took a Thalys train from Brussels to Cologne and changed to an Intercity-Express from Cologne to Berlin. Although she had never taken a train trip across two countries on her own, the trip was a breeze compared to the complexity of her feelings about Guy. She knew it was time to put aside her fears about discussing her life to clear the air with Guy. But what price was she willing to pay to preserve this new friendship? Did she even want to continue it, and more importantly, did she want it to grow into something beyond friendship?

Nora knew instinctively that she hadn't dealt with her feelings about Mitch. Taking on another significant other seemed premature, but did Guy expect it? Would he be satisfied with just being friends? The coward's way of dealing with Guy was to let time and distance resolve the situation. She'd have to return to the US in a month or so and could avoid seeing Guy until then. But for once in her life, she didn't really want to do that. But what did she want to do?

She unlocked the door to her flat and dumped her bag on the couch. She heard a rustle behind her. She whirled around as Michael emerged from her bedroom. "Michael! You scared me! What are you doing here?"

"Thanks, Mom. It's good to see you too," Michael responded, his retort dripping with sarcasm.

"Oh, Michael, of course I'm glad to see you!" Nora gathered her oldest son in a warm embrace. "But is something wrong? I had no idea you were thinking about coming to Germany." *More to the point*, she thought to herself, *I didn't think you had any interest in coming to Germany.*

"Oh, Mom, you're the only one I could talk to about this. Kelly and I broke up!" The anguish in Michael's voice was uncharacteristic. Michael was her sunny son—always upbeat, always positive. It took a lot to upset him. He seemed determined never to allow anything or anyone to, as he put it, "rain on his parade."

"What happened?" Nora asked, as she gently guided Michael to the couch.

"She said that I've changed since Dad died, that I've become sullen and withdrawn. She says she doesn't know me anymore."

"Well, of course you've become withdrawn. Your father died. It was awful for you. It was awful for all of us. What did she expect?"

"I think she thought I'd just get over it and be able to move on after a month or so. But, Mom, I just can't do that. It hurts too much."

"I know it does, sweetheart. I feel the same way."

"Do you really? Kelly says you got over it right away, so why can't I?"

"Michael, Michael, I didn't get over it. I'm still not over it. I don't know if I'll ever get over it. Without your father, I'm not very good at 'getting over' anything!"

"He did sort of make you face things, didn't he? Really, he didn't let any of us get away with much, did he?"

"I used to call him 'the bulldozer' when he'd yammer at me to deal with something I didn't want to face. But I've discovered that I don't know how to do it without him."

"Is that why you came all the way here? Uncle Cary thought you might be hiding out."

"You talked to Cary? When?"

"I called him from the airport. He came and picked me up. Then he talked the lady downstairs into letting me into your apartment. I've been here since yesterday."

"Why didn't Cary call me to let me know you were here?"

"He said he tried, but your phone kept going to voice mail."

Nora fished her cell out of her purse. Seven missed calls from Cary. She remembered she'd shut off the ringer before going to dinner with Guy on her last night in Brussels.

"I'm so sorry, Michael. I wasn't thinking. I turned the ringer off and forgot to turn it back on." In the midst of her ruminations on the train back to Berlin, receiving calls on her cell had been the furthest thing from her mind. "Your uncle is wrong, though. I'm not hiding out. I'm right here, morbid thoughts and all. But we're going to figure out all of this together. I promise you. And Michael . . ."

"Yes, Mom?"

"There's nothing wrong with you for being sad over your dad. Kelly is not the right woman for you if she doesn't understand that."

"Thanks, Mom."

Nora and Michael talked well into the night. Nora discovered that she was able to talk with Michael about some of the things she'd avoided talking to Guy about. Maybe in her role as mother, she could put aside some of her own fears to quell her son's. Whatever the reason, she was grateful. The words, so long held back, flowed from her—not a torrent but more than a trickle. Although it wasn't her intent, helping Michael deal with his feelings helped Nora begin to deal with hers.

Nora yawned as the sun began to rise. "Should we try to get some sleep or would you like some breakfast?" she asked a sleepy Michael whose yawn matched her own.

"I'm tired, but I don't want to sleep yet. My nights are all messed up from jet lag. Can we eat something and then I'll think about sleep?"

"Sure. Let's go downstairs and see what Ilsa has for the breakfast group."

"Who are they?"

"You'll see. Come on. I think the restaurant should be open."

It was, and the first few members of the breakfast group straggled in. Nora did her best to introduce her son to the older men in the group in her broken German. They had softened their attitude toward Nora and condescended to respond in equally broken English. They all chatted somewhat amiably, munching on croissants and *Brotchen* (hard rolls) with strawberry *Marmeladen* while savoring Ilsa's rich dark coffee.

In a flurry of German chatter, Katya and Paula burst through the door. "Chow! Chow!" they called to everyone as they hurried to the counter to survey Ilsa's baked goods. After choosing two gooey chocolate eclairs, they settled in with the group, eyeing Michael with undisguised curiosity.

"Paula, Katya, this is my son Michael. Michael, these are my friends Paula and Katya."

Michael raised a questioning eyebrow. He was obviously taken aback by Nora's choice of friends.

"When did you get here?" asked Paula.

"The day before yesterday. I've been staying in Mom's flat upstairs."

"I don't know how we could have missed that. We're here every morning."

"This is my first time in the restaurant. I felt a bit funny coming down here by myself, so I just ate at Mom's, although she didn't have much in her itty-bitty fridge."

Herr Zimmermann looked puzzled. "Funny? *Lustig?*"

Nora chuckled. "No, not *lustig*—funny-amusing. More like funny-odd or funny-embarassed or self-conscious."

"Ah. *Ich verstehe* (I understand). *Danke.*"

"Did your Mama tell you about the concert we all went to? Flinging Mary?"

"Oh my gosh, Mom. You went to a Flinging Mary concert? That group is wild! I bet you were the only one there over—"

"OK, Michael. We don't need to get into that now."

Michael looked amused. Maybe this visit would be fun. Katya and Paula looked like girls that knew how to have fun. After questioning them about their jobs and where they lived, Michael suggested they all get together after work for coffee.

"Mom, what do you think? Want to join us?"

"No thanks. I think I'll go over to Cary and Monika's and see what they're up to. By the way, there's a beautiful new Starbucks in Zehlendorf. That's a good place to meet. I can tell you how to get there from here if you're interested."

"That sounds great. We'll see you there about six, Michael. *Tschuss*, everybody!" With that, Paula and Katya burst out the door in the same mad swoop with which they'd come in.

"Flinging Mary concerts and trips to Brussels with mystery men. Mom, what's come over you? You've never done that kind of stuff before," Michael said later when they were back in Nora's flat.

"I'm glad I can still surprise you. Now, how about a nap? *I* could certainly use it."

"I'm not sleepy anymore. I think I'll go for a walk. How far is Zehlendorf? I'd like to see this Starbucks you mentioned."

"It's really too far to walk. You can catch a bus a few blocks up the street—bus number 486. It stops right in front of Starbucks. The fare is two euros."

"OK, Mom. I'm off!"

Nora took a short nap—only a half hour or so—then brewed herself a cup of strong black tea. She was just sitting down to a snack of tea and toast when the unmistakable sound of a police siren got louder and louder, then stopped in front of the restaurant.

She ran to the door to find a chagrined Michael on her doorstep with a member of the Berlin Polizei standing next to him.

"Michael, what happened?" she asked. Without waiting for an answer, she turned to the police officer, "*Was hat passiert?*"

"I speak English, madam."

"Mom, why didn't you tell me I needed to pay more when I catch the bus from here? I gave the driver the fare you told me to give him, but I think he kept saying he needed more. It was all in German, so I didn't understand. He got really mad and yelled for the cops who were parked at the corner. He told them I was disrespectful."

"Madam, let me explain. You live in area C, just outside Berlin. The bus fare is another one and a quarter euros outside areas A and B. The driver didn't understand that your son doesn't speak German, and because they were both shouting at one another, he thought your son was refusing to pay the extra fare. Perhaps the driver was hasty in calling for us. It was simply a misunderstanding."

"Can I pay the extra fare for him now?" Nora asked.

"I never actually got on the bus, Mom, so don't give them any money."

"Technically, your son attempted to violate the *Fahrschein* (transportation) rules, so I had to pick him up. But there will be no penalty."

"Thank you so much, officer." Nora sighed with relief.

"Yeah, thanks, I guess," said Michael, not willing to concede that he might have been in the wrong, however unknowingly.

A small crowd had gathered on the sidewalk outside Das Süße Leben. "I saw it all," an old man said. "The boy did nothing wrong."

"Yes, sir," said the police officer as he climbed inside his van. "Good day, madam," he said to Nora with a tiny bow.

"Michael, I'm so sorry about that. To be honest, I've never paid the extra fare. I thought it didn't really matter."

"Well, it obviously does if the driver wants to be a prick about it."

"Please, Michael, watch your language. Hey, I've got an idea. I have to go into Zehlendorf to buy some bread and vegetables. How about we ride the bus together and I'll pay the fares for both of us. What do you say?"

"OK. Let's go." Crisis averted. Michael was happy again. Nora's tea and toast would have to wait.

Later that day, after mastering the bus route to Zehlendorf, Michael left to meet Paula and Katya. Nora savored the silence in her tiny flat as she thought about Michael's encounter with the Berlin police. Michael had not been the easiest child to raise. Always among the smartest in his class, Michael was often bored in school. Unfortunately, there were few programs for gifted students in their school district, and all had long waiting lists. So Michael entertained himself and his classmates with the kind of flippant remarks that drive teachers crazy. In middle school, he gravitated toward the students who came from the town's scruffier neighborhoods. Many of his friends were the children of Mexican migrant workers who came to the Midwest to pick corn or fruit in the rich farmlands of rural Michigan.

Michael began dabbling with drugs and alcohol at fourteen. By the time he got to high school, the local police had picked him up several times for "minor in possession" violations. At sixteen, he'd only driven the family van for a few months when he got his first drunk driving ticket. On his second drunken escapade, he drove into a tree, then Michael threw sand on the smoking engine of Nora's beloved red Chevy Malibu. ("He blew up the mother ship," as one of her students facetiously described it.) After that, Michael was forbidden to drive either Mitch's or Nora's cars.

When Michael first hit his teen years, he and Mitch were often at each other's throats. They once had an actual physical fight on the front porch, with Mitch screaming "get out" and Michael holding onto the porch railing with a death grip—determined not to get out but, rather, to get *into* the house where he'd spent so little time as an adolescent. Nora shivered as she thought of the incident.

Michael had always had a knack for pitting Nora and Mitch against each other. In retaliation, Mitch steadfastly espoused his own brand of "tough love." He'd say to Michael, "We totally support you when you do good things, but when you screw up, you're on your own." Michael would then harrumph at what he termed Mitch's "glib parent-talk."

Nora, on the other hand, was Michael's confidant. He spoke longingly with her on his seventeenth birthday about living on his own. He'd heard about becoming an emancipated minor from a friend at school and thought it sounded great. Nora nodded noncommittally, determined not to make fun of the idea knowing it was something Mitch would never agree to (and of course, neither would she).

By the time Michael reached his junior year in high school, his path toward graduation was strewn with many D's and F's and a smattering of A's in Art. Michael was a talented artist. "He came out of the womb sketching," Nora used to tell her friends. He was constantly drawing the world around him. One unusually supportive teacher arranged a private showing of Michael's sketches at a local gallery in exchange for Michael achieving perfect attendance in his class. Michael's pattern was to sleep in until after Nora and Mitch left for work, miss all his morning classes, then rush off to school to Art every afternoon.

Nora finally caught on to this when she met the high school principal at a parent-teacher conference. Mrs. Cooper, the principal, warned Nora that Michael would not pass most of his classes because of his poor attendance. She showed Nora a record of all the phone calls her office had made to the family phone to report Michael's class absences. Nora noted the phone number. It was not for the family phone. The number listed was for Michael's private phone line, something Nora had given in on after Michael's constant pleading for more than a month. Michael's line was installed over Mitch's adamant objections. When Nora told Mitch about the principal's phone records, she had to reveal to him that the private line—installed initially to free up the family phone—had been used to divert the school's calls away from Mitch and Nora.

That was the final straw for Mitch. Michael was on court-ordered probation by this time. The school had notified Michael's probation officer about his truancy, and an officer showed up at their door to take Michael to jail. Mitch let him. That's the way Nora had seen it at the time—Mitch "let him." Her heart broke, but she refused to visit Michael during his ten days in jail. Mitch visited him every day.

Convinced that Michael's truancy was alcohol-related, Mitch arranged to place Michael in a substance-abuse treatment facility. This turned out to be the turning point in Michael's young life. He took the GED while in the program, passed with flying colors, and was accepted for admission at the local community college after his treatment.

Once in college, Michael never looked back. After community college, he moved on to a nearby university where he earned a Bachelor of Fine Arts degree in Graphic Design. He quickly found a job at a small PR firm. Nora was troubled about what might happen to Michael's job after this sudden trip to Berlin. How to stop worrying about Michael was something with which she had never come to grips. "I guess Cary was right about my hiding out from at least *some* things," she though ruefully.

Trevor and Michael were extreme opposites. Where Michael was sunny and sweet, Trevor was pessimistic and sarcastic. Michael liked his current job. He didn't aspire to make a lot of money or to climb any corporate ladders. Trevor was a "glass half full" kind of guy, always assuming there was more out there—more money to be made, more status to achieve, a more satisfying romance to be found with a woman yet to be discovered. Mitch and Nora agreed that their sons complemented each other perfectly. Mitch used to say that Trevor would pay for their nursing home, but Michael would come to visit them.

Despite his grouchiness, Nora saw Trevor's soft side every once in a while when life disappointed him and he turned to his mother for consolation. "He has that in common with his big brother," Nora mused. Nora was still thinking about the differences between her two sons when Michael burst through her front door. "Mom, I've met the most incredible woman!"

"Paula or Katya?"

"Oh, neither of them. Don't get me wrong, they're both pretty cool, but they have boyfriends—although I think Paula's relationship is pretty shaky from what she told me. No, this other person is a woman named Kelly. Some coincidence, huh?"

"Is she German?"

"No, actually she's American. She's here doing some research here on something she called 'third-generation guilt.' She has this theory that Germans who were alive during World War 2 don't feel nearly as guilty about the Holocaust as their grandchildren. These grandchildren love their grandparents, but they feel guilty for loving them because they suspect—or they *know*—that their grandparents did nothing to help the Jews or maybe even actually did stuff to hurt the Jews."

"That sounds fascinating. Where does she go to school?"

"This is the most amazing part, Mom. She goes to the University of Michigan! She's a grad student in their Communication Department. This research is for her doctoral thesis."

"Even more fascinating. Did you meet her at Starbucks? Was she interviewing someone there?"

"I don't think she had a formal interview going. She was talking to some old guy from Belgium, but he left after a while."

"Some old guy from Belgium," thought Nora. "Three guesses who that was."

"Yeah, I talked to him for a little while too. He seemed nice, and his English was really great. Hey, Mom, can I use your computer? I'd like to check my e-mail."

"Sure, go ahead. I was thinking about walking over to Cary and Monika's in a while. Want to join me?"

"No, I think I'll stay here. I'm still kind of tired."

"OK, then I guess I'll go now before it gets dark."

"Oh, Mom, by the way, I asked Kelly if she wanted to have dinner with us tomorrow night. Is that OK?"

"Sure. Why not?"

As she walked to Cary's, Nora examined her feelings about Guy being back in Berlin. "I really owe him a phone call. Maybe he'd like to have dinner with us tomorrow night." She promised herself she'd call him from Cary's.

Guy gladly accepted Nora's dinner invitation although he seemed surprised to hear from her. Didn't he know that she'd get in touch with him sooner or later? Guy suggested they have dinner at a restaurant in Cary's old neighborhood, not far from the Schlactensee, one of Berlin's many small lakes. Coincidentally, the restaurant was also one of Nora's favorites. On a crisp autumn night, it was a great place to dine alfresco under the stars with a bubbly glass of prosecco to warm her insides.

The next day, Nora she took Michael on a whirlwind tour of the city she loved. They had breakfast at Potemkin, a Russian restaurant in Viktoria-Luise Platz, named after Princess Viktoria Luise of Prussia. Born in 1892, Viktoria was the daughter of Kaiser Wilhelm II of Germany and the great-granddaughter of Britain's Queen Victoria. After breakfast, Nora and Michael hopped on a train which took them to the Brandenburg Gate, the iconic tourist hotspot in Berlin. Michael was awestruck by the size of the quadriga atop the gate but less impressed by the Starbucks directly opposite.

Glancing around the square, Michael asked, "Hey, isn't that the hotel where Michael Jackson dangled his baby out the window?"

"Yes, that's the Hotel Adlon. It's very fancy and very expensive."

"Should we have dinner there tonight?'

"Are you paying?"

"Yikes. I guess we'd better settle for someplace a little less impressive!"

Nora and Michael then took another train to Wittenburg Platz across from KaDeWe. Nora wanted to show Michael the department store's food floor with its amazing array of sausages. "Not the worst place for *wurst* I've ever seen!" quipped Michael. Nora groaned.

Michael insisted on treating Nora to lunch, so she suggested they stop at a German fast-food stand (an *Imbiss*) across from KaDeWe—a far cry from the elegant food floor, but the flatbread sandwich they shared (called a "Doner") tasted wonderful to Nora. "Mmmm," she said, licking the garlic sauce from her fingers.

"Gosh, Mom, you've got to be the cheapest date in Berlin. That whole meal cost me a whopping six euros!"

"But I got to share it with you. That made it really special."

They finished their afternoon at what Nora and Cary had come to term "the apple strudel place" in tiny Lichterfelde West, two train stops from Zehlendorf.

"Mom, this is incredible!" Michael explained between bites of warm strudel, ice cream dripping down his chin.

Nora looked up regretfully from her plate. "I shouldn't be eating this. I just had strudel a few weeks ago. Oh well, I guess I'll have to start wearing my pants with the elastic waist."

"I really didn't need to hear that, Mom. Now that picture is gonna be stuck in my head for the rest of the trip."

As she chatted amiably with Michael, Nora realized that she'd been lonely without her boys. She had a comfortable give-and-take with both of them. After the boys grew up, on the rare occasions when she and Mitch were able to get both boys together, they found so much to laugh about. Michael was adept at egging Trevor on. Trevor normally took himself very seriously, but when he was with Michael, the two of them kept Nora and Mitch in stitches. As the only female in the family, Nora was often the butt of their jokes, but she didn't mind. When they were all together, she'd look around their small circle and think, "We made these wonderful men." She knew Mitch felt the same way.

No father was more proud of his children than Mitch. He never said it, but it was clear from the way he attempted to forge links with both his sons. However, *his* way was not Nora's way. Mitch would slip into "sports talk"—what Nora thought of as his male bonding ritual—whenever he chatted with either of them. "Why do you waste precious time with them talking about the Lions or U-M football? Why don't you ask them about their lives or just tell them you love them?" Nora had suggested to Mitch more than once.

"This is how *I* say it," Mitch would always respond. Nora wondered if Michael and Trevor knew that was what Mitch was saying with all of his talk about football stats and the rehashing of various games.

Unaware of the hour, Nora and Michael meandered back to Nora's flat just before Kelly's arrival. Nora excused herself to take a quick shower. She found Michael and Kelly deep in conversation about Mitch. "I feel like I was just getting to know him. I was such an asshole as a teenager. I don't know how he put up with me. When I finally decided to grow up, he'd already been diagnosed with colon cancer. We had so little time after that. He was a great guy, although I'm not sure my mom always saw him that way."

Nora pretended she hadn't heard the last bit about her feelings about Mitch. "Hello, Kelly! I'm Michael's mom." Nora thrust out her arm, and Kelly jumped up to pump Nora's hand enthusiastically.

"Hi, Dr. Reinhart. It's so nice to meet you," Kelly gushed.

"Please, sit, and it's Nora. I'm only Dr. Reinhart in the classroom."

Kelly was tall—almost six feet of gorgeous blondness. She had a sweet bow-shaped mouth and brown velvety eyes. It did not escape Nora that Kelly bore a striking resemblance to Nora herself, thirty years earlier.

The first Kelly had been a squat redhead with a tendency to whine. Nora tried to like her but found she had a hard time getting beyond the belligerent edge of the nearly continuous demands she made of Michael. ("Michael, sweetie, can you get me my sweater? It's a little chilly in here." "Michael, sweetie, could you hand me another piece of bread. The crust is a little tough on this piece." "Michael, sweetie, could you check the oil in my car? I think it's a teeny bit low since you drove it so much last week.") "Good riddance," Nora thought to herself. "This one seems much nicer."

Nora and Guy had arranged to meet at the restaurant. Rather than the bus-to-train route a trip to the restaurant in Schlactensee normally entailed, Nora sprang for a taxi. Consequently, they arrived well before the time she and Guy had agreed to meet.

"We're a little early, but this gives us a chance to get to know each other," Nora said to Kelly as they settled into their table on the restaurant's patio just outside the front door. It was a beautiful fall evening, unseasonably warm without a hint of the chill the previous days had held. Nora glanced at the menu but already knew what she wanted—a glass of prosecco and the house salad of roasted vegetables and lightly grilled salmon on a bed of dark greens.

"Let's wait until Guy gets here to order our dinners, although I could use a drink now," Nora said, looking pointedly at the nearest waiter.

A few minutes later, as they settled in with drinks and the complimentary bruschetta, Nora got down to the business of exploring Kelly. "So tell me all about your research."

"Well, I'm majoring in communication studies at the University of Michigan. My coursework includes studying both German language and German culture. I'm researching what I call third-generation guilt. I've talked to quite a few young Germans in their teens and twenties, and their general feeling is that the Holocaust is something they will always have to deal with. They feel a great deal of anguish that their country could do something like that. They are proud to be German, but they feel they can't express it because of what happened during the war. They know they're not responsible, but they still see it as their legacy. They seem very frustrated by it all. More than anything, many of the young Germans I talked with want to look at the Holocaust objectively without it being shoved down their throats."

"But who is 'shoving it down their throats'?" Nora asked.

"German schools, for the most part. Ironically, it's seldom talked about in their homes. Outside of Germany, though, that's a different story. I talked to several students at Freie University here in Berlin who were exchange students at US high schools. One guy told me that when he would tell American kids where he came from, they would often say something like 'Isn't that the country

Hitler came from?' Or they would even do the 'Heil Hitler' salute to him. This student from Munich told me he had to keep telling them that neither he nor his parents had anything to do with the Holocaust. He was angry that he had to have these conversations over and over with Americans."

"Another student at Freie I talked with had a different take on it. She told me that she didn't see these kinds of conversations as a burden. She saw them as an opportunity. She felt that Germans can't deny what happened, but people her age have to make sure it doesn't happen again."

"Other students," Kelly continued, "complained to me. 'Why can't we stop talking about the Holocaust?' 'Why can't we talk about what's happening today like the failure to stop genocide in Rwanda or Darfur?' One student said he tries to put the German guilt in perspective by recognizing that even today, people are tolerating mass slaughter.

"Constantly apologizing for the sins of the past can get old, and many young Germans want to engage with the international community without the shadow of the Holocaust looming over them. But precisely because these young Germans feel they are expected to perform some sort of 'penance'—a continuous 'mea culpa,' if you will—they've also become adept at picking out undertones and recognizing exculpatory rhetoric."

"Wow," breathed Nora. "That was amazing."

"Gosh, I'm sorry," said Kelly, blushing deeply. "I get caught up talking about this. That's it. I'm done. Let's talk about your research, Nora."

"Yeah, Mom, are you actually doing some research here?"

"Yes, but it's not really very remarkable. I'd much rather hear about Kelly's. I have a few questions, Kelly, and then we can talk about my modest little research project. First, so how do these kids sort out their feelings about their grandparents who lived through the war?"

"Well, they love them, of course—for the most part—but they struggle with how they can possibly care about someone who might have collaborated with Hitler against the Jews. From the outside, the third generation has had it all—prosperity, access to education, peace and stability—but they also grew up with a lot of unspoken secrets in their families. Often, if they asked questions, they're given vague answers or told to 'leave well enough alone' or 'don't poke around in things that don't concern you.' Some of them try to find out more by doing their own research, hoping they won't find anything about their family members."

"Why did you pick this subject?" Nora asked.

Kelly looked down. Nora thought she seemed to be grappling to find the right words. "Well, I was noodling around on the Internet about a year ago and found an article in the online edition of the British newspaper, *The Morning Tribune*. There was no author cited for the story—I don't know why—but the details in the story about the reactions of grandchildren of World War 2-era Germans really intrigued me. After I read it, I decided I wanted to explore the whole thing myself."

"Can you tell us about one of these grandchildren?" prompted Michael.

"Sure. One woman—her name is Uhla Wascher—found out that her grandfather was the most dreadful torturer at Bergen-Belsen. She was reading books about the Holocaust for a university class and read about her grandfather in one of the books. She said she felt numb for days after she read about what he'd done. For many years, she was ashamed to tell anybody about him, but then she realized that her own silence was eating her up from inside. Her grandfather, Wilhelm Wascher, invented what's known as 'the Wascher swing' at Bergen-Belsen—an iron bar that hung on chains from the ceiling. Wascher would force naked inmates to bend over the bar and beat their genitals until they fainted or died.

"The article said it took Uhla several years of therapy and group seminars to even begin to come to terms with the fact that her grandfather was a monster. She felt guilty for what he'd done, even though she hadn't committed a crime herself. She felt like she had to do only good things all the time to make up for her grandfather. She had never personally met her grandfather. He died in prison in 1970. After her father died five years ago, she found old letters from her grandfather from prison, begging to see his grandchildren—but that never happened.

"Uhla told the author of the article that her grandfather killed a little boy on one of the transports to Bergen-Belsen who had an apple by smashing his head against a wall until he was dead. Then he picked up the apple and ate it. Ironically, he later put a picture of Uhla as a little girl over his bed in prison. How is she supposed to come to terms with all that?"

"Good evening, everyone," said Guy as he greeted the three who sat in stunned silence. "Am I late?"

"No, no. You're right on time," Nora assured him. "Kelly was just telling us about her remarkable research project."

"Yes, it is remarkable, isn't it? She was talking to me about it yesterday when I met her at the Starbucks in Zehlendorf. It seems that everyone is doing some sort of research these days."

"Hello, sir. I'm Nora's son. It's good to see you again," said Michael politely as he held out his right hand for a handshake.

"Hello again. Michael, is it? I would like to say I've heard much about you, but I have not."

"I'm not surprised. Mom can be pretty closed-mouthed sometimes."

"Closed-mouthed? I don't think I know what that means."

"Well," explained Michael, "it's not really secretive, but it sure isn't very revealing."

"A very apt description of your mother!" Guy said with just a hint of sarcasm.

"Now that Guy is here, shall we order?" Nora quickly changed the subject as she directed another "come here" look at a nearby waitperson.

The evening passed uneventfully. Nora managed to steer the conversation away from herself every time Michael said something that could be construed as too personal. Statements that began with "Mom always . . ." and "You know what Mom did when . . ." were deflected with "Now, Michael, nobody wants to hear about that." Secretly, Nora was starting to think that her attempts to keep her secrets—whatever they were—were coming across as somewhat pretentious. "A woman of mystery" was simply not a role she normally sought. But she was afraid that once she began talking about her parents or Mitch, like Pandora's box, she'd never be able to tightly snug the lid back on again.

Guy spent much of the evening entertaining them with stories of his childhood with the Runeberg family in Sweden. He made their coldness seem almost comical. "Their idea of a wonderful birthday gift was to give me a new pen or a pair of woolen sox. Something practical was always the most efficient way to get the most out of what they thought of as an essentially frivolous occasion. My sister thought this was hilarious. As an adult, she sent me a pair of sox every year for my birthday. After the first few years, these sox grew more and more outrageous. Once, she actually managed to find a pair of green-and-red plaid. That was my sister. She simply couldn't be practical. It just wasn't in her nature." Guy's angular face softened when he talked about his sister Lillet.

"Somehow I doubt that happened when Mitch talked about me," Nora thought.

"The Runebergs were not unkind. They were just old-fashioned. They came from a time when it was held that children should remain out of sight as much as possible. So Lillet and I spent much of our time in our rooms. Mrs. Runeberg's cousin had given her an old train set her son had lost interest in, so we set it up in my room. The train came with a station in a tiny village we named Liegeville for the city in Belgium we came from. We pretended that our papa was the engineer and our mama was a rich lady with her own personal train car with red velvet seats and angels painted on the ceiling. Sometimes this fancy lady would invite us to ride with her. She would tell us wonderful stories about a magical kingdom of toys that came alive at night and played funny tricks on the boys and girls who owned them.

"Of course, it was really Lillet telling me these stories. My favorite was about a mischievous doll who hid one shoe from each of her owner's three pairs of shoes. One pair of shoes was really too small. So the little girl who loved her doll so much was left with one black ballet slipper and one heavy rubber boot of a type

I think Americans referred to years ago as a 'three-button Arctic.' Off to school the little girl went. There was no end to the mockery in that child's classroom for days until the missing things finally turned up."

Kelly was enthralled by Guy's stories about him and his sister. Throughout the evening, Nora watched Kelly out of the corner of her eye. She sensed there was something disturbing Kelly about her own family life despite her aura of American-Midwest wholesomeness. "There's a darkness surrounding her too," Nora speculated.

Michael, on the other hand, was full of light and enthusiasm. The emotional storm that landed him on German shores had passed. He seemed totally comfortable with both the company and the atmosphere. "What a beautiful night," he exclaimed, stretching luxuriously.

"It is indeed, but I have to get up early for another interview tomorrow," said Nora, "so we need to call it a day."

"Will you need my services tomorrow, madam?" asked Guy with mock formality.

"No, but you're welcome to come if you're interested. I'm interviewing an old friend, Stefan, who grew up in the former East. His English is excellent, but you might enjoy hearing his story. I suspect it will be quite different from those we've heard so far."

"Then tomorrow it is. How is nine at your flat?"

"Perfect. I'll see you then."

Guy and Kelly headed for Guy's car. The trip to Kelly's flat required two train changes and a wait of at least twenty minutes on the Yorckstrasse station platform, so Guy had offered to take her home. Michael and Nora opted to walk to the Schlactensee train station. The train to Zehlendorf was due in ten minutes. Another expensive taxi would take them home from there.

*   *   *

Kelly shared a flat with another American student in Mitte on the edge of the Kreuzberg district in Berlin. The flat was large and airy, with two comfortable bedrooms and a huge double living room. It overlooked a courtyard five stories below. Unfortunately, the pre-war building had no elevator, so once she was out and about every day, Kelly avoided going home and climbing the endless stairs until absolutely necessary. Consequently, she sought out good hangout spots all over the city, which had brought her to the Zehlendorf Starbucks.

Kelly grew up in a warm loving family in the upper peninsula of Michigan with two brothers and a sister. Her father worked for the state forestry service. Her mother was a teacher at the local elementary school. But her picture-perfect childhood was colored by a secret her father had hinted at but never disclosed until just before Kelly began her graduate studies. All of her life, she assumed this secret had something to do with her grandfather.

Her grandfather—always referred to in the family as "Opa"— came from Germany. That much Kelly had always known. Her grandmother died shortly after she and Opa came to the United States after the war. Opa was not a shy man, but he seldom said much about his life in Germany. Instead, he talked often about how much better his life was in the US.

Among his three grandchildren, Kelly was Opa's favorite. "How Oma would have loved you, Kelly, with your beautiful blond hair and your sweet smile. On the other hand, the boys would have made her laugh with the way they wrestle like little bear cubs. Oh well, at least she was here for a little while." His voice trailing off, he'd sigh wistfully.

On the rare occasion when he'd talk about Germany, he'd describe the green forest and the clear stream near his home. "Sometimes we'd fish in the stream, my sister and I, and we'd catch dinner for my mama. Those were good days." Again, the sigh.

"But, Opa, why did you leave Germany if it was so nice?" When she was little, Kelly would ask him this after each brief recollection.

"It's too hard to explain. Some bad things were done, and your Oma and I just wanted to get away."

Kelly stopped asking about Germany, fearful that her Opa had done these "bad things." A few years after she'd started college, she found out the truth.

Opa was in the hospital. He'd had a series of heart attacks, and it was clear he wouldn't survive the last one. Kelly's dad was the last family member to talk with Opa. The truth finally came out. Oma and Opa had left Germany because of something someone else in the family had done—someone who was seldom spoken of, someone whose name no one in Kelly's immediate family knew until that day in Opa's hospital room.

Opa's sister (whom Opa had always referred to as "Sissy") had brought—as Opa described it—"great shame on the family." As she grew older, it was clear that she was not the innocent Opa knew as a young girl. "Sissy" became a bully. As a young teenager, she was tall and heavy, with a thick neck and hands and feet that were bigger than those of most of the boys in her class. The boys in town gave her a nickname she hated—*die fette Kuh* (the fat cow). They would follow her home after school, mooing, until Sissy ran far ahead, out of sight and hearing range.

It would be easy to say that her size and the teasing made her what she later turned out to be, but the truth was, Sissy was mean. When others teased her, she teased Opa. She was always bigger and stronger than he was and delighted in twisting his arm until he screamed or whipping him with a ripe young bough from the willow tree in front of their house. Opa never told his mother or father about these incidents for fear Sissy would be punished and later launch an even more vicious attack against him. He'd seen this happen at school.

The adult Sissy retained the ugly mean-spirited character of the adolesecent Sissy, but she later directed her hatefulness toward others even more defenseless than her little brother.

Kelly's father beleived that the rest of the family was entitled to know the truth about what had been kept secret for so many years in the Heim family. The family name was actually not "Heim" but "Heimernacht." Sissy's full name was Elva Heimernacht. She was employed as a guard at the Nazi concentration camps of Bergen-Belsen and Auschwitz and was later a warden of the women's section at Buchenwald. Heimernacht was convicted for crimes against humanity at the Belsen Trial and sentenced to death. Executed at twenty-one years old, "Sissy" was the youngest woman to die under the jurisdiction of an English court in the twentieth century. She was nicknamed the "Beast of Buchenwald."

Opa and Oma left Germany shortly after the execution. This was all Opa told Papa on his deathbed. It was enough for Papa but not enough for Kelly.

Finding out more was easy in this day of the Internet. It took no time at all for Kelly to find this entry on a German history website:

> Elva Heimernacht was born to Alfred Heimernacht, a dairy worker and a member of the Nazi Party from 1936, and Berta Heimernacht. Elva Heimernacht had three siblings. Heimernacht left school in 1938 at the age of fifteen, owing to a combination of a poor scholastic aptitude, bullying by classmates, and a fanatical preoccupation with the League of German Girls (*Bund Deutscher Mädel*), a Nazi female youth organization, of which her father disapproved. Among other casual jobs, she worked as an orderly in the sanatorium of the Secret Service for two years, after which she worked on a dairy farm.
>
> Quoted below is Elva Heimernacht's testimony, under direct examination, about her background:
>
> "I was born on 7 October 1924. In 1938 I left the elementary school and worked for six months on agricultural jobs at a farm, after which I worked in a shop in Bohmshof for six months. When I was 16 I went to a hospital in Retzow, where I stayed for two years. I tried to become a nurse but the Labour Exchange would not allow that and sent me to work in a dairy in Neuthymen. In July, 1942, I tried again to become a nurse, but the Labour Exchange sent me to Bergen-Belsen Concentration Camp, although I protested against it.

I stayed there until March, 1943, when I went to Auschwitz. I remained at Auschwitz until January, 1945."

Having completed her training in March 1943, Heimernacht was transferred as a female guard to Auschwitz and by the end of that year was *Senior Supervisor*, the second highest ranking woman at the camp, in charge of around 30,000 Jewish female prisoners.

In January 1945, Heimernacht briefly returned to Bergen-Belsen before ending her wartime career at Buchenwald as a *Work Service Manager* from March to April, being captured by the British on 15 May 1945, together with other SS personnel who did not flee.

Heimernacht was among the 44 people accused of war crimes at the Belsen Trial. She was tried over the first period of the trials (September 17 to November 17, 1945) and was represented by Major Richard Ivanson.

The trials were conducted under British military law in Lüneburg, and the charges derived from the Geneva Convention of 1929 regarding the treatment of prisoners. The accusations against her centered on her ill-treatment and murder of those imprisoned at the camps, including setting dogs on inmates, shootings and sadistic beatings with a whip. Survivors provided detailed testimony of murders, tortures, and other cruelties, especially towards women, in which Heimernacht engaged during her years at Auschwitz and Bergen-Belsen. They testified to acts of sadism, beatings, and arbitrary shootings of prisoners, savaging of prisoners by her trained and allegedly half-starved dogs, and to her selecting prisoners for the gas chambers. After a fifty-three day trial, Heimernacht was sentenced to hang. Witnesses testified that Heimernacht used both physical and emotional methods to torture the camp's inmates and enjoyed shooting prisoners in cold blood. They also claimed that she beat some women to death and whipped others using a leather belt.

Heimernacht and ten others (eight men and two other women were convicted for crimes against humanity in both

Auschwitz and Belsen and then sentenced to death. As the verdicts were read, Heimernacht was the only prisoner to remain defiant; her subsequent appeal was rejected.

On Tuesday, 11 November 1945, Heimernacht was led to the gallows. The women were hanged singly first and then the men in pairs. Regimental Sergeant-Major O'Brian assisted the noted British executioner, Austin Crowley:

". . . we climbed the stairs to the cells where the condemned were waiting. A German officer at the door leading to the corridor flung open the door and we filed past the row of faces and into the execution chamber. The officers stood at attention. Brigadier General Martin Evans stood with his wristwatch raised. He gave me the signal, and a sigh of released breath was audible in the chamber. I walked into the corridor. 'Elva Heimernacht', I called."

"The German guards quickly closed all grills on twelve of the inspection holes and opened one door. Elva Heimernacht stepped out. The cell was far too small for me to go inside, and I had to pinion her in the corridor. 'Follow me,' I said in English, and O'Brian repeated the order in German. At 9.34 a.m. she walked into the execution chamber, gazed for a moment at the officials standing round it, then walked on to the center of the trap, where I had made a chalk mark. She stood on this mark very firmly, and as I placed the white cap over her head she said in her deep voice, 'Schnell.' (quickly) The drop crashed down, and the doctor followed me into the pit and pronounced her dead. After twenty minutes, the body was taken down and placed in a coffin ready for burial.

Kelly read this entry many, many times. Each time she hoped to find some redeeming quality in her great-aunt, but there appeared to be none. She struggled with how she should feel about this distant relative. Should she feel sad? She knew she was appalled, even repulsed, but was there another emotion this revelation should generate? For the most part, she felt nothing, and this emotional numbness grew more distressing to her every day.

When Kelly was faced with choosing a topic for her doctoral research, the concept of third-generation guilt came quickly to mind. Although she told Nora she chose the topic because her interest was piqued by the article in the online *Morning Tribune*, the truth was that the article simply provided additional support for what she already knew she wanted to research. Perhaps in studying what others had experienced, she could find out how she should feel about her aunt, Kelly reasoned.

She was less interested in the horror stories of ancestors who had collaborated with, or were part of, the Nazi regime. What she hoped her research would identify was any common threads in the reactions of grandchildren to their grandparents' actions during the war. For example, if she found that most descendants felt remorse and a strong sense of guilt, that would tell her how *she* was supposed to feel. Not the best reason for chosing a research topic, but Kelly knew from talks with other grad students that personal interests often influence the choice of what to study, especially in her field where much of the research was interpretive. Quantitative research was usually left to the "hard sciences" of biology, chemistry, or physics.

So Kelly set about lining up interviews with young people in Germany. Her roommate who was studying at Berlin's Freie University had also agreed to help Kelly find German students willing to be interviewed. Language differences didn't pose much of a problem. German had always been spoken in Kelly's home out of deference to Opa, but all of the students she'd interviewed so far had studied English in school and were anxious to try out their English skills with a native English speaker.

*   *   *

Kelly peered squinty-eyed down the long stretch of road. Far ahead, a huge crowd of people emerged from the forest and ran onto the road. Although they were still some distance from her, they rapidly narrowed the divide. As they came closer, Kelly turned and ran, but they were clearly gaining on her. She braced herself for the hands that would grab her and drag her down and the brown-booted feet that would trample her prostrate body. The first of the runners was now so close, she could feel his hot breath on her neck. But he didn't stop. He and the others ran past her, dressed in the same drab clothes of dung-colored homespun. Each carried a weapon of sorts. Some carried pitchforks; some carried hoes or other primitive farming tools. Kelly fell in line near the end of the group. She looked down and saw that she was clutching a scythe and dressed in the same ugly clothes as the others. They ran on. Kelly sensed their mission and accepted it.

Kelly woke with a start. "What a dumb dream, " she thought, refusing to acknowledge the fearsome message of the dream. But she knew what it meant: *you are one of us.* She turned over and tried to go back to sleep, but the message of the dream replayed over and over in her sleep-starved brain.

*   *   *

On the other side of the city, Nora struggled to stay awake. She had fallen into a frustrating pattern—avoiding sleep and the inevitable dreams until the first light of dawn. Exhausted, she would then slip into a deep, dream-free slumber to wake late in the morning feeling hot and lightheaded. In the hours before she succumbed to sleep, she replayed conversations she'd had with Mitch.

She had often accused him of being obsessively self-centered. "I'm so tired of coming in second place with you!" she'd rail. But looking back, she realized that what she saw as self-centeredness, Mitch termed "self reliance." He was the youngest of four children, born of a working mother who was over forty when he was born. It was a time when mothers rarely worked outside the home and seldom had children so late in life. Her mother-in-law once told Nora, "Mitch grew up in spite of us." This neatly captured the state of benign neglect in which Mitch was raised.

In one of their many arguments on his "selfishness," Mitch denied that he hardly ever considered Nora's wants and needs. "I think about you all the time—I think about how *I* fit into all your little routines and rituals. Our social life together centers on *your* friends and what *you* like to do (which is mostly shopping)," he'd said with a little half-smile.

"You like to shop as much as I do, maybe more," Nora retorted, thinking of all the times she'd spent waiting for Mitch in a cafe at their local mall.

"I shop a lot because *you* do, and anyway, I don't buy much. I mostly look—you know, 'comparative shopping.'" Another small smile.

"If you're 'mostly looking,' why are you always exchanging things?"

Always, never—Nora's side of most arguments was peppered with generalizations, according to Mitch. Nora maintained that he refused to see the patterns in his behavior. And so they went on through the years, indulging in what Mitch once called "recreational fighting." Neither was willing to accept that he or she might be wrong. In fact, such a premium was placed on being right that Trevor had come up with a name for his parents' sparring—"Peabody-ing"—after "Mr. Peabody," a cartoon dog who educated "his boy Sherman" via a time-traveling device called the "way-back machine."

"Where are we going today, Mr. Peabody?" the bespectacled Sherman would ask.

"Today we're traveling to Mesopotamia, the cradle of civilization," was a typical Mr. Peabody response. Mr. Peabody's view of the world, both past and present, was always correct—and so too, they both thought, were Nora's and Mitch's.

Mitch had always insisted that their different approaches to life (and there were so many!) were simply a matter of what he called "style points"—but Nora, not surprisingly, saw it differently. Although she never told Mitch this, she secretly thought there had to be plenty of "Mr. Wonderfuls" out there with whom she could have had a far better, or at least a more tranquil, life.

Did this mean she hadn't loved him? She wasn't sure. They used to joke about occasionally feeling "swooney" about each another, but was that really love? Mitch maintained that love is a commitment, but that sounded to Nora about as romantic as a business contract. But then, she also suspected she wasn't really a romantic anyway. It was all so confusing to Nora, and she was no closer to understanding her feelings about Mitch than she had been when he was alive.

She forced herself to think about the good times with Mitch. She knew she was being ridiculous when she answered her own unspoken question with "what good times?" A picture of two young people in their twenties swam before her eyes. They sat on a log in a clearing in the woods surrounded by the vivid reds and golds of October leaves. His hair was windblown, with a hint of silvery highlights. She wore a soft denim hat and held a cluster of pussy-willow branches—his first gift to her. They had gone "up North" to that part of Michigan north of Traverse City that always felt a little untamed and mysterious. They camped in Wilderness State Park in a tiny tent with her puppy Zoe yipping and whining all night long. Nora remembered lying beside Mitch in the sleeping bags they had zipped together, feeling a rare moment of joy as pure and effervescent as a glass of champagne. "I'm actually really and truly happy with this man," she had marveled.

Then Mitch had sneezed, a honk so loud Nora could feel the sound vibrating down the length of her spine. "Sorry," Mitch had mumbled. Over the years of their married life, Nora swore that Mitch sneezed at least a dozen times a day. Always the same obscenely loud trumpeting. Each time it happened, she wondered how she could tolerate it for even one more day.

A few months after that first camping trip, they decided to marry, although neither had much money to speak of. To pay for Mitch's wedding band, Nora sold a beautiful crystal pendant with a silver filigree overlay and a single perfect diamond her grandmother had left her. She often thought longingly about that pendant. Nora never did find out how Mitch paid for her ring.

They went together to a wholesale jeweler in Detroit to pick out their rings. They opted for the same gold bands—wide, with five rows of ridges in the middle separated by small upraised dots. They had to special-order the bands. But when the order arrived,

Mitch's band turned out to be narrower and in white gold, and Nora's was the original wider band in yellow gold. It was three days before the wedding, so they opted to keep the bands despite the mistake in their order. The matched/mismatched bands became a symbol of their uniquely different takes on the same subjects in their marriage.

The wedding itself was another matter entirely. No white dress with five bridesmaids, crazy bachelor parties, or a multi-tiered wedding cake for Nora and Mitch. Nora wanted the wedding to be an event they both could plan, an event memorable for its simplicity. Although the relatives on both her mother's and her father's side had always been married in big Catholic church weddings, Mitch and Nora were married in a civil ceremony in a courtroom in Hazel Park, Michigan. The ceremony was so brief, Nora hardly had time to take off her coat. Behind them on the benches in the courtroom sat the participants in a trial scheduled immediately after the wedding (a child custody case, Nora later found out).

A dinner for twenty friends and family members followed the ceremony. Mitch's best friend offered to be their photographer as his gift to them but later misplaced the undeveloped film. Only two snapshots of their wedding existed, taken by Cary with his tiny Instamatic, slightly out of focus, showing Nora with a deer-in-the-headlights look that said "What have I done?" (Or so Nora later interpreted it.)

One thing she knew for sure: this trip to Berlin hadn't helped. Oh, she still enjoyed the city, but she couldn't shake the bone-chilling loneliness she had come to associate with being alone in Berlin. Having Michael with her helped, but it didn't dispel the fear that being by herself, living out the rest of her life alone, was a destiny she was ill-prepared for.

Nora's friend Cele who had never married once told Nora, "I'm alone, but I'm not lonely." Nora aspired to feel the same sense of satisfaction with life on her own but feared it would always be beyond her.

*   *   *

Nora and Guy arrived at Stefan's flat shortly after 9:00 a.m. Stefan was ready for them. He had been looking at photos taken during his first trip to the West after the Wall came down. He recalls being a typical teenager then—his thoughts full of "girls, girls, and more girls." Like most people in Germany, Stefan was actually asleep when the first flood of people from the East entered West Berlin. He told Nora that the night before, he had watched a press conference on TV that started it all. An official from the government of East Germany called the press conference to announce the lifting of many travel restrictions for East Germans who wanted to travel in the West. When asked when these changes would take place, the speaker seemed dumbfounded and, without official permission, said "immediately." This was the signal for East Germans to "storm the gates."

Stefan went to school the day after the Wall came down, but there was no actual instruction in his gym class. His teacher had gone to the West the night before. He told his class all about it while his students stood around and marveled. Stefan and two of his friends decided that they too would go to the West right away. Stefan had accidentally left his house keys at home, so he had to go to his mother's office to get a second set. His mother begged him not to go to the West, but he went anyway. At the checkpoint at Bornholmerstrasse where he was to meet his friends, Stefan saw a line of people so long that "it was impossible to see the end." One of his friends joined him, and while they waited for another friend, a second gate opened and many of the folks in line streamed into the West, Stefan and his friend among them. Stefan recalled running for fear of getting trampled by the sea of people behind him.

His first reaction when he saw the west side of Bornholmerstrasse was that it looked just like the east side— gray and depressing. His first act in the West was to go to the nearest bank to collect his "welcome money"—one hundred deutsch marks. For years before the Wall came down, a few East Germans—Pensionärin (retirees) and others with special permission—were allowed to collect this princely sum courtesy of the government of West Germany. This could only be done once a year, though. Although the incredible number of East Germans swarming into the West threatened to break the banks, Stefan and his friend collected their money with little trouble and surprisingly little time "in queue."

Stefan and his friend went to the nearest tobacco shop to buy "sweets" and were amazed by the bright colors of the packaging, the displays, and even the clothing Westerners in the shop wore. In East Germany, colors were always subdued—grayed and washed out. Stefan was also amazed by the quantity of newspapers and magazines. In the East, there were only a few of each at the newsstands. When Nora asked Stefan whether the Wall coming down was a good thing, he thought for a moment.

"At first, I thought it wasn't because of the speed with which reunification occurred. But now, in retrospect, I think that it couldn't have happened any other way. People in the East wanted change immediately. The fall of the Wall was only one of a number of events leading up to this change. To postpone it for long would have been inappropriate," he concluded. Looking nervously around him, Stefan told Nora and Guy that the Communist regime in East Germany was repressive and needed to be eliminated, but he didn't believe that most East Germans had necessarily been dissatisfied with their lives. The country they lived in, after all, was all they knew. To spend every day wishing for something different would have made daily living impossible, according to Stefan.

Nora and Guy exchanged looks. On the surface, Stefan's observations weren't all that different from Mari's, but it was clear that their views on Reunification were very different—even polar opposites.

"That's not to say that East Germans didn't know that there were other ways of living in the West. Many of us were able to watch Western television—although it was illegal to do so— and a few of us were even allowed to buy Western products at selected stores in the East. Pepsi, for example, was licensed to sell its products in these stores."

"Despite living in East Germany, I had a very happy childhood," Stefan added. "But the fall of the Wall changed my life dramatically. In the East I was 'delegated' to go to a specialized technical school for further education after tenth grade. This program would not have allowed me to take the German *Abitur* (the test that, if passed successfully in several different areas of study, leads directly to university for most students)." When the Wall came down, Stefan was able to continue in school on a path that led from the Abitur to university where he graduated with a degree in marketing. He boasted that he'd traveled around the world, even lived in Ireland for a year. He marveled at the people he's met, people he never would have known if he had lived the life he was programmed to live in East Germany. Remarking on the concept of "the Wall of the mind," Stefan said that although Germany is united now, many of his friends from the old East never leave their eastern neighborhoods in Berlin. For them, the Wall is self-imposed.

*   *   *

"Mom? Are you OK? You've been sleeping all morning." Michael bent over her, gently shaking her arm, his face scrunched up with concern.

"I'm fine. I just had trouble sleeping last night, so I guess I was making up for it this morning. How long have you been up?"

"Hours. Kelly came over and we had Frühstück downstairs."

"Frühstück, huh? As opposed to breakfast?"

"When in Rome . . ."

"So what are your plans for the day?" Nora asked as she sat up, propped up her pillow, and settled in for a chat.

"I'm going to a lecture at Freie University with Kelly. In fact, I have to hurry. She's meeting me at the S-Bahn in twenty minutes. I just came back for my train pass."

Nora's face fell. She'd hoped to spend the day with Michael. "Have fun," she said quickly to mask her disappointment.

Another long day with little to do. She could call Guy, but she wasn't sure she wanted to encourage him. Nora was sure that was what a phone call could do. She sensed that Guy's feelings for her were changing—deepening—ever since the day he joined her for her interview with Stefan. The interview went well, but Nora vowed to keep her interviews with Guy present infrequent enough to discourage intimacy. But her resolve was weakening in the face of her loneliness.

She suddenly had an idea. She'd been promising herself for weeks that she'd go to Alt Tegel in the far northeast of Berlin to visit Marta, the sister of Nora's friend Tomas. Tomas had been a visiting scholar in the Math Department at the University of Michigan. A mutual friend had contacted Nora and asked her to help Tomas get settled in the US. She and Mitch had happily done so after meeting Tomas at the airport. Young and full of energy, Tomas had been the breath of fresh air they needed after Mitch had first been diagnosed.

Marta had visited Tomas shortly after he'd arrived in the US, and together, they hosted a small dinner party for Mitch and Nora and a few of Tomas's new math colleagues. Marta was a self-confessed workaholic, finishing a residency at a Berlin hospital before joining her father in his internal medicine practice. All this fell by the wayside, however, when Marta met Hans on an Internet dating site. Within a year, they had traveled around the world together, gotten pregnant and married (in that order), and bought a beautiful home not far from Tomas's and Marta's parents.

Marta was now a happy stay-at-home mom in Berlin with one-year-old Asa. Nora was curious about how Marta's transformation from doctor to hausfrau had taken place so quickly and, seemingly, effortlessly. Time to find out.

Perhaps Cary might join her. Before he met Monika, he had briefly dated Marta before pronouncing her "too focused on her career."

Unfortunately, Cary had an all-day teacher in-service, so Nora was on her own again. A bus and a long train ride later, she stood in front of one of the most beautiful houses she'd seen in Berlin. She rang the doorbell that sounded a lot like the chimes on a Berlin tram.

Marta answered the door with Asa in her arms. "It's so wonderful to see you again! Come in!" she said in German. Nora stared in awe at the domed ceiling in the living room and the wall of glass through which a proper English garden was in full view. While studying for a year at Oxford, Marta fell in love with the beautifully groomed gardens of England and decided that if she ever had a home of her own, she'd try to replicate what she had so enjoyed in England.

"I remember how much you like *Spargel* (asparagus), so I made *Cremespargelsuppe* for us. Asa is still on the breast, so he won't be joining us," Marta said as she planted a soft kiss on Asa's dark hair as his eyelids drooped to half mast. "Just let me put him down for his nap and then we can talk."

This gave Nora a chance to take a closer look at Hans and Marta's living room. Tomas had told Nora that Hans designed the house, but she was not prepared for the sweeping vista through the living room windows and the impressive use of glass and chrome— clean and simple and surprisingly warm, not at all the cold, stark feel this combination often produces. "Guy would love this," Nora knew instinctively.

Nora and Marta spent the afternoon catching up. They hadn't seen each other since before Mitch's death. Nora accepted Marta's condolences but changed the subject quickly to Marta 's new role as wife and mother. "I always saw you as married to your career."

"I saw myself that way too," Marta admitted. "But when I met Hans, all that changed. I know it doesn't sound very liberated, but I feel more myself than ever before."

"Oh, I plan to go back to medicine when Asa starts school, but right now I am completely satisfied. Asa takes up much of my time, and Hans—well, you have the perfect expression in English to describe him. He's my 'soul mate,' just as Mitch was yours."

Nora almost choked on her coffee. "I definitely wouldn't describe Mitch that way."

"But he was, Nora. Tomas and I would often say you and Mitch had the perfect marriage. Even after so many years together, you always had something to say to each other. You never seemed bored with Mitch, or he with you."

"Well, that's true. I never thought of it that way. To his credit, I did see him as my intellectual equal. In fact, I have to admit that I expended a lot of energy trying to prove I was smarter than him. I used to think of it as intellectual jousting, but I think Mitch just saw it as me being argumentative." Nora admitted this with the same quirky half-smile she'd seen on the Mitch in her dreams.

After promising to get together with Marta again soon, Nora began the long trip back to her flat. On the way to her train, something peculiar happened. Nora stumbled several times as she climbed steps to the train platform. Suddenly, she was aware of a dark band over her right eye. She blinked several times. It was still there. "I'm just tired," she reassured herself. Then she remembered that she'd poked her eye rather decisively with her mascara wand while putting on her makeup before the trip to Marta's. "That must be it," Nora concluded and dismissed the matter for the moment.

But when Nora woke up the next morning, the dark cloud over her line of vision was opaque. She had a sinking feeling that she knew what it was. When she was in her midtwenties, the retina in her right eye had torn. Although the distortion was a little different this time, the sensation of trying to peer over something that she couldn't blink away was the same. Fighting off panic, she phoned Monika. "I'll call my eye doctor right away. Maybe she can see you today."

Not surprisingly, Monika's ophthalmologist, Dr. Richter, suspected a serious problem when Monika described what Nora was experiencing. She agreed to see Nora as soon as Nora could get to her office. Unfortunately, Cary had taken his car to work and Michael was nowhere to be found, so Nora was left to find the doctor's office on her own. Although she'd never before used the particular bus route to Dr. Richter's office, a burst of adrenalin drove her until she found the unfamiliar bus line.

Once at Dr. Richter's office, a huge sheaf of paperwork needed to be filled out before she could see the doctor. When Nora finally settled in for the exam, it quickly became clear that her premonition about what had happened was dead-on.

"You must get to the hospital for an operation right away. Your condition is very serious," Dr. Richter said solemnly after what seemed to Nora a rather cursory exam. "I will cancel my patients and drive you there myself." Now Nora was really scared. No doctor in the US would ever agree to drive a patient to the hospital (ooh, the liability!).

After another hurried phone call to Monika, Nora found herself in Dr. Richter's black Mercedes convertible, speeding to Berlin's *Sankt Gertrauden Krankenhaus* (St. Gertrude's), the nearest hospital with an eye clinic.

Dr. Richter deposited Nora in a worn leather chair in the eye clinic's waiting room. She then explained Nora's situation in hushed tones to the receptionist. Nora sat very still. German voices swirled around her. Her mastery of the simple German words for "she" and "eye" and "problem" were lost in waves of panic. What if she lost the vision in her right eye? Could her "good eye" compensate sufficiently? Would she still be able or read, or would one of her greatest pleasures be lost forever?

A tear trickled down her cheek, followed by another. Dr. Richter pulled a straight-backed chair next to Nora's and reached for Nora's hand in one smooth motion. "Do not be afraid. The doctors here are among the best in Germany. The chief surgeon, Dr. Chen, has performed this surgery many, many times—and always with good results," Dr. Richter assured Nora in her stilted English.

Right on cue, a tiny Asian man rushed into the waiting room, followed by a host of acolytes in white coats. "Good morning, Frau Reinhart. I am Dr. Chen. I will examine you now, but from what Dr. Richter tells us, you will need surgery right away."

Despite her fears, Nora stifled a giggle. It tickled her to hear German spoken with such a strong Asian (Chinese?) accent. Unfortunately, Dr. Chen spoke no English, so Nora was back to relying on her *kinderlich* (childlike) German to explain her symptoms as well as her medical history.

Dr. Chen's exam confirmed that the retina in her right eye had indeed torn again. He patiently explained that not until he began the operation would he be able to determine whether a small bubble of gas injected behind the retina would be sufficient to fuse the edges of the tear together. In the worst cases, the balloon needed to be filled with silicone oil rather than gas. The primary difference between the two approaches was in the recovery time. At best, Nora would need to remain in Germany for at least three weeks before flying home. At worst, maybe as long as six weeks. It hit Nora that she wanted to get home more than anything in the world: home to the familiar, home to friends and her students, home to her husband . . . She stifled a sob. There was no husband to go home to.

If Mitch were alive, he'd be beside her, holding her, whispering reassurances. "You can do this, sweetheart. Try not to worry. I'll be with you right up to the time they take you in for the surgery, and I'll be there waiting in the recovery room, bed pan at the ready." This made her smile. That's exactly what Mitch would say if he were still with her.

The next twenty-four hours flew by in a blur. Before the surgery, Nora had to meet with someone in the hospital's billing department. She had failed to buy the travel insurance Mitch always insisted on, so she was forced to use her credit card to prepay for the surgery and her hospital stay—four thousand euros in all (a fraction of what her insurance would have paid for a similar procedure in the US). With her credit card maxed out, Nora was checked into a double-room (empty because her roommate was mysteriously "walking the hospital grounds," according to the floor nurse who repeatedly addressed Nora as "Frau Reinhart"). She drifted off soon after, sleeping fitfully until dawn when it was time to be prepped for surgery.

The next thing she knew, Nora awoke to find three concerned faces hovering over her. "Wake up, Frau Reinhart. Your operation is over. Wake up, please," said an unknown male voice in German who turned out to be the recovery-room nurse.

"Hey, Mom, are you OK?" Michael's face registered the most concern.

"Sure, she's OK, Mikey. Your mom's a warrior. She's going to be fine," said Cary, attempting to reassure Michael while massaging Nora's arm gently.

"Monika and Guy are here too," added Cary, "but they would only let Mikey and I come into the recovery room."

"Guy is here? But why?" Nora said groggily.

"Because he was worried about you. We all were." Michael's tone suggested that she should know they would all be there for her.

"Mmmm . . . that's nice," whispered Nora as she dozed off again.

*　　*　　*

Guy stood at the foot of Nora's hospital bed, feeling uncharacteristically indecisive. He held a huge bouquet of roses in his right hand and a tiny white box in his left. He was tempted to leave his gifts on Nora's bedside table and slip out unnoticed. Instead, he promised himself he would leave as soon as Nora woke and he could see for himself that she was all right.

Guy hated hospitals. They were the setting for some of the worst moments of his life. The way he saw it, bad things started and ended in hospitals. He couldn't remember receiving any good news about his wife in a hospital, only grim predictions that always came true.

He tried to brush these thoughts aside and concentrate on this other woman lying in a hospital bed. She was not his wife. She was not suffering from a life-threatening illness. She was a friend, although Guy was not really sure how good a friend she was. Perhaps he should leave after all and check in on Nora after she'd had a chance to recuperate in her flat. He turned to leave.

"Guy?"

"Nora, you're awake." Guy hurried to her bedside. "How are you feeling?"

"I've had better days," Nora said wryly. "But I'm OK. Are those for me?" she added, indicating the flowers and the tiny box with a small nod of her head.

Guy smiled. This was the Nora he'd come to know. So straightforward about some things while holding back on so many others.

"Yes, of course. Michael told me you love yellow roses. They are not so easy to find in Berlin."

"And the box?"

"This is a special gift for you. Something to keep you safe. I hope you like it. It belonged to my sister. I found it among her things yesterday. I think she'd like you to have it." Guy placed the tiny box in Nora's hand.

Despite Dr. Chen's cautions about sitting up too soon, curiosity got the better of her. Plumping her pillows, Nora rose to a sitting position. She lifted the lid of the box. Cushioned in light blue satin was a silver Star of David with a tiny diamond in the center of of its six points. It was suspended from the most delicate silver chain Nora had ever seen.

"Guy, this is so beautiful. Are you sure you want me to have it?"

"Yes, I am. It suits you well, I think."

"I'm not sure I know what the Star of David actually means. Can you tell me?"

"The meaning is not completely certain. Many very strict Jews believe that the six points on the star represent God's absolute rule over the universe—north, south, east, west, up, and down. Others believe that the two triangles that form the star signify the dual nature of man, good and bad, and the star is a protection against the evil spirits that can overcome the goodness in humanity.

"There is also a Jewish legend about King David and the star," continued Guy. "It says that when David was a young man, he fought his enemy King Nimrod. The shield he took into battle had two interlocking triangles on a round base. The battle became so intense that the triangles fused together. David won the battle, so the star that formed was forever after known as the Star of David."

"Wonderful! Do you think if I wear the star every day, it will keep me from any more harm?"

"It can't hurt," Guy responded with a shrug.

Nora hooked the chain around her neck and straightened the star as it lay on her well-worn hospital gown. She promised herself she'd never take it off.

*   *   *

Three days later, she was dressed and ready to leave the hospital. Michael, Cary, and Guy were engaged in some sort of conference in the hall outside her room. Nora couldn't hear what they were saying, but they clearly had come to an agreement.

"What's up?" she asked Michael as all three filed into her room.

"Mom, you really can't go back to your flat right now. We talked to your doctor, and he said that even though he didn't have to perform the surgery with the oil bubble, you will still need to be very careful for at least three weeks. You can't lift anything heavy, and no reading or computer. You need to keep your head down most of the time, so no TV either. So we don't see how you can do much for yourself."

"You are always welcome to stay with us, but Monika has to travel a lot this month and I have a full schedule of classes, so there'll be nobody at our house most days during the week," Cary said. But he quickly added, "But we think we have a solution."

"I would like it very much if you would come and stay at my sister's—*my* house," Guy said quickly, anticipating Nora's objections. "I have a housekeeper, as you know. Even though she's not always so pleasant, she is a very fine cook, and I like to think I am good company enough to make up for Helena."

"But, Michael, can't you take care of me?"

"Oh, Mom, I'm so sorry, but I have to get back home to work. My boss e-mailed me yesterday and said that If I don't come home soon, I won't have a job to come back to."

"But what about Kelly?" Nora said a bit desperately. More time with Kelly might be the enducement Michael needed to stay in Berlin.

"Kelly is going home to the States in a few weeks. We'll see each other again when she gets back at school. Meanwhile, we'll Skype and e-mail every week just like you and I do. And, Mom, if you're still here at Christmas, I promise I'll try to come back. Maybe Kelly could even come with me."

"Oh, Michael, I hope to be home long before Christmas," Nora assured him.

Guy's face fell. Nora talked so little about home and family, he'd somehow convinced himself she'd be staying in Berlin indefinitely. Apparently, that wouldn't be the case.

"It looks like I don't have a choice. Guy's it is."

"I promise it won't be painful," Guy said. "You might even enjoy yourself."

"Oh, Guy, I didn't mean to sound ungrateful. I just don't want to be any trouble."

"I assure you, you won't be."

The short drive to Guy's drained Nora of every last drop of her diminished reserve of energy. Bone-tired from the effort of playing the good patient, never complaining, always cheerful and cooperative with a hospital staff that spoke almost no English, Nora longed for nothing more than a comfy bed with no guardrail.

Helena greeted Nora at the door with her starched apron and a sour look that said "no sympathy here." Guy ignored her and guided Nora to the guest room.

"*Schlaft gut* (sleep well), Nora. I'll see you in the morning," Guy said as he softly closed the door.

Nora gratefully climbed into bed and quickly fell into a deep sleep.

*　　*　　*

After seeing Michael off at the airport on her third day at Guy's, Nora and Guy's relationship settled into a gentle, comforting rhythm. Like Nora, Guy was an avid reader who shared her interest in literature about Germany and the Holocaust. They began with *The Book Thief*, one of Nora's favorites. At first they listened to the audio version of the book but when the second CD began to skip every few minutes, Guy simply picked up a hard copy of the book and took over as narrator, his deep baritone filling the room with rich expression. Nora sighed contentedly as the last sentences of Zuzak's remarkable book faded away.

"Tomorrow I have another very special book for you. It's called *Those Who Save Us* by Jenna Blum. It's about a woman in Germany who worked at a bakery and stuffed bread into the trees in a nearby wood to save the Jews who were hiding in the forest. They called her 'the bread angel,'" Guy said.

They worked their way through Blum's book, followed by Eli Wiesel's *Night*, and Erik Larson's *In the Garden of Beasts*. Guy's voice never faltered although he read to Nora for hours on end. There was something so intimate about being read to—"almost as intimate as sex," thought Nora wryly. But there was also a sweet innocence to it. It made her feel safe again, just as she'd felt when her mother read to her every night before bed as a little girl. But that was before she found out the truth about her parents.

Nora was now convinced that she knew the truth about Guy. Her instincts told her that he was a kind, caring man capable of both great generosity as well as righteous anger when it came to protecting those he loved. In many ways, he reminded her of the four men she was closest to in her own family—Mitch, Michael, Trevor, Cary—who had loved her and cared for her without reservation. Nora decided that although he made no demands of her, Guy deserved an honest hearing from her regardless of any reciprocal "strings" that might be attached to his confession.

"Guy," she said, after dinner on the third Sunday of her stay at his house. "Can you tell me what happened with your wife?"

"Of course, Nora. I've wanted to tell you about her for a long time, but you never seemed interested." Guy waited for a sign that Nora was really ready to hear his story. She placed her hand over his and gave it a brief squeeze. That was the sign Guy needed.

"Anais was the great love of my life. She was all I ever wanted in a wife. She was beautiful, but more importantly, she was very intelligent with a wonderful sense of humor. She and my sister were close friends. When the two of them got together, they were so amusing. Anais was particularly clever at imitating some of my clients whom she found particularly egotistical and stuffy. She and Lillet fed off one another. One would tell a joke, and the other would try to outdo her. There was always much laughter in our home when Lillet came to visit.

"Anais was an only child, so more than anything, she wanted children of her own—and lots of them. After three miscarriages, we had to face the reality that there was something wrong with one or both of us. Of course, this was in the days before genetic testing, so we never discovered the source of the problem. Although we did not want to give up hope, the doctors told us that Anais likely would never successfully carry a child to term.

"But we had each other and the company of other people's children. Anais performed volunteer work in Belgium for a relief agency for African immigrants. She was always inviting 'her families' for dinner and sometimes overnight if they had no other place to go. There were many children in these families. Anais was never happier than when our house was filled with children's voices.

"We had a good life until Anais got sick. At first, we were optimistic that she would get better. We had a wonderful doctor, Alan Duval, who was a longtime friend of my aunt's. Unfortunately, he died soon after Anais was diagnosed, but not before he sold his practice to another doctor, Martin Zanger. To this day, I have no idea why such a fine man as Alan would have any relationship with a demon like Zanger.

"We had a great deal of difficulty getting an appointment with Zanger, and when we finally did, he insisted that it wasn't necessary for Anais to have radiation or chemotherapy. Without treatment, Anais deteriorated rapidly. When she was hospitalized for the last time, another doctor at the hospital—an oncologist—told us that if Anais had received treatment right after her diagnosis, there was a good chance that she would have lived much longer, perhaps for years. When I confronted Zanger, he denied that he had ignored the severity of her condition. Two days later, he managed to get the oncologist fired from the hospital.

"I again tried to talk to Zanger, but he refused to listen. I threatened to sue him, but he denied all responsibility. He flew into a rage and began saying things like 'You people think you're entitled to special treatment' and, finally, 'They should have gotten rid of all of you!' I shoved him and he fell. He landed very lightly against a padded chair, but later, he told the police that I threw him against the wall. He started wearing a sling and told everyone who would listen that he had dislocated his shoulder and pinched several nerves in his arm from the fall. He called it an 'attack,' which was truly laughable.

"He filed charges against me, and the police arrested me the day Anais died." Guy's face contorted with the raw rage that had overtaken him on that horrible day. His beloved Anais was gone with no time for him to mourn her passing. He deeply resented being required to defend his reactions to Zanger's negligence to the Brussels police even while a private memorial service for Anais was being held.

"Oh my god, Guy, that's so terrible!" Nora knew intimately what it felt like to deal with two conflicting emotions at the time of a loved one's death—grief over the loss colored by a red-hot anger over the circumstances surrounding the death.

"Then I did something I'm not proud of. No one else knows this, Nora, but my closest friend in Belgium. This friend was acquainted with the judge assigned to my case, Michel Vervouve. He and Vervouve had been lovers before Vervouve became a judge. I told my attorney about this, and he told Vervouve that I would reveal the truth about his homosexuality if he did not dismiss the charges against me. Vervouve was terrified that the truth about him would come out. He was married to a woman from a very prominent family in Brussels, and the story would have caused quite a stir. As I said, I'm not proud of using his personal life against Vervouve in this way, but it worked. Vervouve agreed to dismiss the charges but demanded that I leave Belgium immediately. This was around the time when I found out that Lillet was sick, so I had even more reason to leave the country. So I left Belgium and came to Berlin. You know the rest of the story from there, Nora.

"We all do what we must to survive. I learned that early in life," Guy added. "Even as a small child, I knew that my parents would never have turned their children over to someone else if they hadn't been worried about our survival. 'Survival' can mean different things to different people. For me, it meant surviving with my dignity, having the opportunity to grieve over my wife's death in private—out of the public eye, as I was in Brussels. I don't think my choice to blackmail Vervouve—for of course, that's what it was—hurt him or anyone else. Zanger never learned about the real reason the charges were dismissed against me, but I heard that he told many people in his circle of acquaintances that it was because Vervouve was also Jewish. 'They take care of their own,' he would say right up to the day he died to anyone who would listen. I had nothing to do with his death. He did it to himself with his ugly feelings about anyone who didn't meet his standards of acceptability.

"Really, the only person who was hurt by what I did was me. I have always prided myself on my integrity. I can now no longer do that. I compromised my personal code of ethics, and that's something I'll live with for the rest my life."

Nora let go of Guy's hand and moved to sit next to him. She found herself stroking his back. She thought deeply about what she could say to this man who had been so kind to her. What could she offer him but her forgiveness?

"Guy, it seems to me that you've spent much of your life being punished for who you are, not what you've done. This Zanger sounds like he wouldn't have been satisfied with however your situation was resolved. You were simply doing what you had to do to take care of yourself, just as your parents did for you when they sent you and Lillet away. We are all allowed to love and care for ourselves as long as we do it without hurting other people. I don't think I ever understood this about my husband. He was very good at taking care of himself, but somehow I thought that meant that this left him with fewer resources to take care of me. I was actually jealous of his feelings about himself."

"It sounds like we both need to first forgive ourselves before we can forgive anyone else," responded Guy. What he really meant was that *Nora* needed to forgive herself before she could forgive her parents or Mitch for any real or imaginary offenses. Guy was too polite to say this, however.

"Guy, now I'd like to tell you about my parents. May I?" Nora asked in the tiniest of voices.

Guy nodded, his smile offering Nora the encouragement she needed.

"I loved my parents so much, especially my father. My mother was wonderful but it was my father to whom I always turned for love and support. With my mother, this was a given. I had to work to earn the love of my father. He was really a demanding man but, like you, he had high standards. I was the oldest child and so naturally my parents had no frame of reference for how to treat me. I think, until Cary was born, they saw me as a tiny adult and judged me accordingly. With Cary, my father was more understanding, but he also seemed to have fewer expectations of Cary. Cary did what Cary wanted. I did what my father wanted. My father was a professor, and he wanted me to be a professor too. As a student at the university, there were other things I would have rather studied like theater or interior design. But my father saw these fields as trivial. His field—Communication—was a serious field of study, as serious as medicine or law in his mind. So I focused on my father's field which, over time, became *my* field—a field I've come to love.

"It was the same thing with my boyfriends. There was a boy I was crazy about when I was around twenty. My father thought he was silly and superficial, so he introduced me to Mitch, who was the son of one of his colleagues in a service club he belonged to. I didn't like Mitch much at first, although I came to accept him eventually, but I think I never forgave my father for trying to break up my relationship with my first love. His name was Charlie. Over the years, I always thought Charlie and I would have been a better match than Mitch and I." Nora shook her head. "But maybe I was wrong.

"My relationship with my father was never the same after Mitch and I married. I felt like my father had turned me over to Mitch and sort of washed his hands of his daughter. In my mind, I know this wasn't true, but my heart thinks otherwise. After years of being number one in my father's eyes, I believed he'd replaced me with Mitch and, later, my children. It was horrible of me to be jealous of my sons for their grandfather's affection. I once tried to talk about this with Mitch, but he told me it was time for me to grow up and give up my role as 'daddy's little girl.' Mitch could be pretty blunt, and perhaps I needed to hear what he said, but at the time, it was simply one more thing to hold against him."

"Was your husband unkind to you, Nora?"

"No, he really wasn't. He was just different from me—or more importantly, different from my father. Cary always says that my father indulged me. This was certainly not true of Mitch. He never let me get away with anything!" Nora smiled ruefully, remembering Mitch's no-nonsense attitude toward her. "'Nora,' he'd say, 'time to be a big girl. You're a grown woman with two children, a PhD, and a husband who needs some attention now and then—so suck it up and give it to me!'

"I wanted to be the wife he wanted, but I didn't know how. I was so used to being on the receiving end of things. I don't think I knew how to be a giver, except to my children. That seemed to come easy. With Mitch, it was all so complicated. I always assumed that Mitch could get along just fine on his own without me. I felt like I was just a passenger on Mitch's little ship of life, and whether I jumped off or stayed on, he'd keep on sailing along one way or the other. I believed he didn't really need me."

"How did your husband die, Nora?" Guy said gently.

"He had cancer, just like Anais, and although he got very good care, the cancer had progressed too far by the time he was diagnosed. He only lived a few months after his diagnosis."

"Did you have a chance to say good-bye to him?"

"No. I was at a conference when he died. Mitch had begged me to go to the conference. I was presenting a paper I'd worked hard on, and he wanted me to have a chance to talk about it with my colleagues. I didn't want to go, but he seemed a little better so I agreed. Trevor called me at the conference to tell me to come home, that his father was getting weaker and might not make it through the week. I got on the first plane, but by the time I got home, Mitch was gone."

"Just like with Lillet."

"There was so much I should have said to Mitch. I wanted to tell him that no matter how much we'd fought over the years, I loved him and I needed him whether he needed me or not. He was my best friend, my sounding board, my conscience, and I treated him so horribly."

Nora's sobs filled the room. She cried for Mitch and she cried for her father, and more than anything, she cried for herself. Mitch knew she loved him and understood that her feelings for him were all tangled up in her feelings for her father.

It was her father that Nora had counted on to always be there for her through childhood, adolescence, and into adulthood. When her father withdrew his affection, her faith in men was badly shaken. Mitch tried to help her see that he wasn't like her father, but she just couldn't believe him.

Dr. Albert Weismer was a simply a little man. He was never the hero, the larger-than-life figure Nora believed him to be. He was a mediocre professor (thirty years of tepid student evaluations confirmed this), an uninspiring scholar, and a self-absorbed husband and parent. Cary saw his father for what he was. Nora saw him for what she wanted him to be. She had convinced herself that her worth could only be established in the reflected glory of Albert Weismer.

Her disillusionment with her father peaked the night of her parents' accident. Mitch was out of town on business. Nora was having dinner with her parents at their request. "We don't get to see you much anymore," her mother had said. "Besides, your father has something he needs to tell you."

There was an odd note in her mother's voice. Something wasn't right, but Nora couldn't imagine what it might be. This was long before Mitch's diagnosis. The boys were still little. Michael's teen angst was well in the future. Nora and her father were actually getting along better than they had in a while. So what was bothering her mother? Nora would soon find out.

They had just finished dinner at her father's favorite restaurant, a place typical of what Mitch called "the feed bag"—family-style restaurants that specialize in meat and potatoes, and lots of them. Nora was not a vegetarian but she ate little red meat, favoring fish or chicken when she had a choice. When her father was around, though, the choices were always made by him. He picked the restaurant as well as the time for disclosing whatever was bothering her mother, even though Nora repeatedly asked her mom what was wrong throughout dinner.

Her father cleared his throat and ceremoniously laid his napkin delicately beside his plate. "Al, is it really necessary to get into all this now?" Her mother was even more agitated. It was clear that her father was determined to reveal something.

"Yes, Ellen, it is. Nora, you know you've always been my number one girl. I'm so proud of you, how you've turned out. You're nothing like your mother."

"Dad, that's a strange thing to say. What do you mean?"

"I'm saying you're more like me than your mother. She was strong-willed and stubborn. Everything was about what *she* wanted, not what was best for you."

"You're scaring me, Dad. Mom, what's he talking about?"

"Your father will explain. It's not my place to tell you."

"Here's the story, Nora. This happened a long time ago. It really doesn't mean much anymore and I never planned to tell you at all, but it looks like I have to now. Years ago, I had an affair with one of my students. She was quite the little tease. She did everything she could to tempt me. She came to my office to discuss every assignment, even the most routine chapter exercises. She gave me little gifts for my birthday and Christmas. She even managed to wangle an invitation to a party at the college president's house, one to which students were not invited but where she knew I'd be. Eventually, I just gave in to her. I want you to know that this was before your mother and I were married."

"Just," her mother said under her breath.

"My student—I don't think you need to know her name— became pregnant. By then, the affair had ended, and Ellen and I were making plans to get married. This student insisted that she was not able to take care of a child. She didn't have the 'resources,' she said. She told me she didn't believe in abortion, so that was out of the question. She had worked it all out. Your mother and I would take the baby and raise it as our own. Of course, I objected. It was *her* mistake, after all. I objected strongly to the entire way she handled it. It felt like emotional blackmail. I told her that I would support her child but that she was responsible for your upbringing.

"But then she threatened to go to the dean and tell him about our affair. The college had a very strict policy against faculty fraternizing with students. I knew if the dean got wind of it, I'd be fired. I told Ellen about what your mother was insisting on, and amazingly, she agreed to it. She saved me and, I suspect, she saved you from what probably would have been a rather sad existence. No mother could have loved you more than Ellen did, Nora."

"Why are you telling me this now, Dad? Why on earth wouldn't you have told me long ago? Whatever possessed you to keep this from me all my life?" Nora's voice grew louder and shriller with each question. Her father hushed her.

"Now, Nora, this doesn't have to be such a big deal. Frankly, I didn't see why you ever had to know, but your birth mother has some sort of condition that could be passed on to you, and she insists that you should know about it. She was determined to tell you herself if I didn't."

"Albert," Nora's mother cut off her father abruptly. Nora had never heard her mother speak so sharply to her father. "I can't believe you are minimizing the situation this way. The woman has breast cancer. She may not live. She also found out that she has the BRCA2 gene, which is a genetic predisposition to breast or ovarian cancer," Ellen explained. "It seems her mother and her sister also had breast cancer. Her mother actually died of it. She wanted us to tell you about this so you can get tested for the gene."

"Dad, how can you treat this so lightly? Not only are you springing a new mother on me, but you're also telling me that I might have some sort of gene for cancer." Suddenly, Nora discovered that the myth about "seeing red" when fierce anger flares up was real.

"And, Nora, there's one more thing . . ." her mother spoke haltingly.

"Oh my god, Mom, what?"

"The fact that two other women in her immediate family have the gene and got cancer increased your mother's risk, and as her biological daughter, it also increases yours." Ellen slumped back in her chair, exhausted from the effort of tackling a subject her husband should have handled better. But why should this be any different from any other difficult situation? He had always left the dirty work up to her. It began with the task—although it soon became a joy—of caring for another woman's child and continued from one challenging situation to another throughout their many years of marriage.

Nora was speechless for a moment. Then it was as if the clouds parted overhead and, for the first time in her life, she saw what a mean-spirited person her father was. "Dad," she said softly, "I don't think I can ever forgive you for not telling me about this sooner." Nora threw her napkin on the table and ran out of the restaurant. She heard her father calling her name. "Nora, Nora, come back here. You're acting like a child. Come back!"

Nora relived the scene in excruciating detail. With a start, she realized that she was no longer in the restaurant with her parents but sitting in Guy's cozy library. "That was the last I saw of either of them. After I left the restaurant, I drove to my friend Cele's house. I just couldn't go home yet. I had no idea that my parents had followed me out of the restaurant. They must not have seen me turn toward Cele's because they were headed toward my house. My mother was driving. The police think she hit a patch of ice and the car spun out of control. She struck a tree, and she and my dad were both killed. The police couldn't reach me, so I didn't find out until much later when I got home and found their message on my answering machine."

"What a horrible way to find out!"

"Yeah, but what was mystifying—truly mystifying—is why my mom was driving. She *never* drove when she was with my father. He always just took his place behind the wheel as if that was just the natural state of things. And I guess for him, it was. Cary thinks my mom was driving because my dad might not have been feeling well, but I think it was because my mom wanted to come after me to try to make things right, and my dad didn't want to. He would have assumed that everything would work out if they just gave it time, but she probably argued with him. She must have beaten him to the driver's seat. Maybe he was pouting when she got behind the wheel. He hated to be contradicted.

"If I had stayed in the restaurant, if I hadn't stormed out like the child my dad accused me of being, they'd be alive today."

"Nora, you can't say that. You reacted as many people would have reacted. You needed to get away from them to process what you had just heard. It was terribly troubling information and not something to just 'work out.' So many times, I have said to myself, 'If only I had noticed that Anais had gotten weaker' or 'If only I had found a new doctor and demanded a second opinion.' If only, if only. You can drive yourself crazy with those two words. Things are as they are. Anais and I had a wonderful life together. It sounds like you had generally good relations with your family. Perhaps that's all we can hope for in life."

"That's where you're wrong about me. My husband and I did not have a wonderful life together. I don't know what it was. Maybe we were just too different. I know he loved me and I think I loved him, but we just couldn't seem to get along. I've thought a lot about it since I've been here, and I think maybe I resented the fact that my father picked out my husband for me. It was almost like a modern American interpretation of the arranged marriage," Nora added wryly.

"Nora, there are many kinds of marriages, perhaps as many as there are people. Every marriage has conflict, and if it doesn't, it's not a marriage of equals. Anais and I had our differences, but essentially, we were very similar in temperament and background. That makes for a more peaceful marriage, but maybe not one with great passion and fire."

"But if my marriage wasn't a bad marriage, then I have so much more to feel guilty about. I treated my husband dismally. My only consolation through the years is that he deserved it, which is silly because he really didn't. His worst offense is that he irritated me. It reminds me of an old situation comedy on American TV where Bill Cosby played a gym teacher in an elementary school."

Guy blinked at Nora's abrupt shift to a new subject. What *was* she talking about?

"Bill Cosby's character had an old aunt and uncle, a married couple played by black actors who both did standup comedy for centuries—Mantan Moreland and Moms Mabley. The best line between them was something I often said to Mitch. 'I only had one nerve left, and you done got on it!'"

Guy guffawed. Only Nora could rise out of the blackest of moods and tell the silliest story he'd heard in a long time. Nora was taken aback by Guy's reaction. Was it really funny? Was it possible that she had taken her constant wrangling with Mitch way too seriously? If that was so, what did that say about her? She just didn't know. She needed to find out though, and soon, because her relationship with Guy was feeling way too intimate.

*　　*　　*

Nora's days at Guy's were peppered with post-op visits to the Sankt Gertrauden eye clinic. Although she was always pronounced to be on the mend, the brief ten-minute exams were prefaced by long sits in the clinic's waiting room. Nora hadn't received the go-ahead to read books or magazines, so she amused herself by deciphering the waiting room's rules. *Immer with the rules in Deutschland,* she thought to herself. No matter where she went, there seemed to be a set of rules—posted in German or simply implied—that always needed to be discovered. She managed to break the code of the waiting room's posted rules after several visits. As far as Nora could tell, many of the rules dealt with civility, stressing the importance of not taking one's frustrations over long waits out on one's companions in waiting-room hell.

The unspoken protocol for waiting-room comings and goings was this: upon entering the waiting room, one must always greet those already present. One *Guten Tag* for all, followed by ten or twelve *Guten Tags* in response. When one leaves after the typical two-hour wait, one must also say good-bye to the waiting-room folks. *Aufwiedersehen* to all with many voices echoing the same. This routine struck Nora as ridiculous. In the US, Nora reasoned, the objective is to get in and out of a waiting room with the least amount of human contact. After all, the waitng room is only a waystation before one's real destination—the meeting with the doctor; it's meaningless in and of itself, a necessary evil of sorts. Why gussy it up with these phony greetings and farewells?

When she was finally examined by Dr. Chen, there was always an akward pause, a waiting-for-the-other-shoe-to-drop moment, after which Nora feared bad news would follow. But the news always seemed good. She found out that the pause might have been because Dr. Chen had observed what her opthamologist in the US would later call "a crinkle" in her repaired retina. This small imperfection caused a slight distortion of the vision in Nora's right eye. Back in the US, Nora's American doctor assured her that this could well work itself out either by her good eye compensating or the tiny fold actually smoothing itself out over time. None of this was explained to Nora in Germany. Her doctor's limited English and Nora's minimal German precluded complex explanations, so she continued to worry before every post-op visit, only to be somewhat reassured until the next visit.

One of the few benefits of the surgery Nora couldn't have predicted was the parade of visitors she entertained at Guy's house. Helena, Guy's surly housekeeper, made it very clear that she didn't appreciate the constant flow of guests even though Nora told her repeatedly not to bother with refreshments other than water or tea. Cary and Monika came often, of course, and even Monika's son Florian showed up several times. Cary's neighbors, the Hochstellers, entertained Nora with their stories about the more outlandish residents of their street in Lankwitz. Ilsa Meijer, Nora's landlady, brought a bag full of Nora's favorite pastries, still warm from the oven. Even Katya and Paula from the breakfast club at *Das Süße Leben* showed up, probably more out of curiosity than anything else. But it was Kelly's visits that proved to be the most memorable.

Nora saw a great deal of herself in Kelly. It wasn't just the physical resemblance. Kelly shared Nora's tendency to steer conversations away from personal information to safer, more neutral ground. But she perplexed Nora. Why did Kelly's research seem so much more "charged" now than it had when she first told Nora about it? For some reason, Kelly no longer wanted to talk about her work no matter how many times Nora asked her about it. She also suddenly seemed reluctant to talk about her family back in Michigan. Nora understood *that*, given her own complex feelings about her parents and Mitch, but why was Kelly hesitant to talk about her research? Unless, Nora speculated, the two were connected.

The Internet had told her much of what she wanted to know about Guy. She could also try googling Kelly's name to see what she could come up with. That seemed so underhanded, though. Unlike with Monika's dire warnings about Guy, Kelly posed no threat to Nora. She supposed she could make a case for a search based on the need to protect Michael from heartache. But Michael was an adult. He didn't need his mommy to look out for him anymore (or at least not in the romance department). Perhaps, Nora reasoned, she should just take the more direct approach as she had when she asked Guy about his wife. But Guy had often suggested a willingness to talk about Anais before Nora's questioning. Kelly did not project the same willingness. Nora finally asked Guy what he thought.

"Nora, I think you'll have to ask Kelly herself. I know what the problem is, but it's not right for me to share it with you. It's Kelly's story, not mine. I can tell you that she discovered something very troubling about her family. She told me about it when we first met in Zehlendorf after she found out I was Jewish. For some reason, she seemed to need my understanding, maybe even my forgiveness. But I assure you, she really has nothing to feel guilty about."

"Now you've really piqued my interest. Do you think I should just ask her about it?"

"What can it hurt? She can refuse, but perhaps she'll succumb to your charm and tell you everything," Guy said with smile.

"I think you overestimate my charm." Nora decided that the next time Kelly came to visit, she'd broach the subject of her research gently in the most tactful way she knew.

*   *   *

"Kelly, I've been thinking about something," Nora said several days later as she and Kelly sipped their tea and savored slices of Helena's grudgingly tendered Black Forest cake. "I still have a few days here at Guy's, maybe even a week or so if my doctor doesn't give me the go-ahead to fly home. I can't read yet, but I would be very happy to listen to your plans for your research or if you're willing to read me what you have so far. I think I can give you some good feedback before you send your first chapter to your dissertation committee in Michigan. What do you say?"

"Oh, Nora, I couldn't ask you to do that."

"Yes, you could. Anyway, you'd actually be doing me a favor. I need to start thinking about my classes for next semester as well as what I want to do with my own research. Hearing about yours would motivate me to get into gear with my academic responsibilities. Please, can't I help?"

"No, really, I'd be boring you. I'd much rather talk about the books you and Guy have read, or maybe you can tell me some more stories about Michael and Trevor when they were little boys."

"Kelly, I really won't take no for an answer. I had a wonderful professor that served as my unofficial mentor when I was working on my dissertation, and I'd love to be that for you."

"Nora, I'm afraid if I tell you the history of my research, you won't want to be involved with me anymore."

"How could your research possibly turn me against you?"

"It's not the research itself. It's what made me want to do the research. It's has to do with my family in Germany."

"I didn't know you had any relatives here."

"I don't now, but I did at one time."

"This all sounds quite mysterious."

"That's not the word I use to describe my family history. I call it disturbing, even horrifying."

"Now I really am interested!"

"Let me show you what I'm talking about." With that, Kelly opened the laptop she always carried with her and clicked on an entry in her bookmarks. "Here, read it for yourself." She thrust her computer into Nora's lap. Then she walked to the nearest window, her back to Nora, with her hands in the pockets of her jeans, head down to hide the tears that slowly drifted down her cheeks.

Nora read the same Wikipedia entry that had been Kelly's introduction to her great-aunt's role as a Nazi concentration-camp guard. When she finished reading, she carefully set Kelly's computer on the table in front of her.

"Come here, Kelly. Sit down next to me."

Kelly reluctantly moved away from the window and sat as far from Nora as the sofa would allow. "I am so embarrassed you read that."

"Kelly, I know you're embarrassed, but I don't think any less of you for having read this about your aunt. Please tell me what you're so worried about."

"Well," Kelly said softly, "first, I'm ashamed that someone in my family hurt so many people. How could she do that? What made her? How could she be so cruel when my grandfather—her brother—was so kind and gentle? Did something happen to her that made her the way she was? I want some answers, but there's no one left to give them to me."

"Then you'll just have to provide your own answers. When you search your heart about this, what are you afraid you'll find?" The pain in Kelly's eyes told Nora that she had hit a nerve.

"I'm afraid that the evil is in me too," Kelly confessed in a barely audible whisper.

"Here's where you need to tell that part of you that thinks you might be capable of the horrible things your aunt did. You are not her. If you inherited anything from that generation, it was the goodness of your grandfather. You told me about him when I first met you—before you decided that what you'd discovered about your aunt needed to be buried within you as your deepest, darkest secret."

"But what if I *am* like her?"

"Have you ever deliberately hurt someone? Have you ever turned your back on someone in pain? Have you ever refused to admit to your mistakes? Even though I don't know you well, I am almost positive that the answer to all these questions is no."

"But how can you be so sure?"

"I'm sure because I think you might be a lot like me—too ready to blame yourself for what other people do. I've done it with my parents' death, and it colored everything else in my life. Don't do what I did. You need to shed this guilt like a snake sheds his skin. Otherwise, you're in danger of destroying a relationship with someone you love, someone maybe, like Michael?"

"Are you saying that I need to tell people about my aunt?"

"You told Guy, didn't you? What did he say about it?"

"I only told him because he saw me reading the Wikipedia article and asked me what I knew about Auschwitz. His parents died there, but he probably told you that."

"Yes, he did, and he told me other things that happened to him—some he's not proud of, but he's learning to separate what was done to him from what he did. That's quite an achievement, I think, but then Guy is an exceptional person."

Kelly nodded in agreement, thinking that Nora, too, was proving to be someone special, though she sensed that Nora was occupied with healing more than her torn retina. Yet Nora's advice to Kelly—to publicly admit her connection to her aunt and her aunt's horrific history—gave Kelly a lot to think about. Her own healing may have begun.

Chapter 11

A t her fourth and final post-op visit to the Sankt Gertrauden eye clinic, Nora got the news that her retina was healing well and it was now safe to fly back to the US. Although she'd been hoping to hear that she could leave Berlin, when she thought about leaving her friends and family in the city, especially Guy, she almost wished she could extend her stay a bit longer. But intermittent hints of an early winter, always dark and gloomy in Berlin, suggested she had reached the inevitable conclusion of her visit.

Nora postponed telling Guy that she planned to leave Berlin. Instead, she invited him to join her for a visit to another of her favorite places in the city: the Gardens of the World in Marzahn. She'd tell Guy about going home then.

As with so many neighborhoods in Berlin, Marzahn began as a tiny village. In 1920, it was annexed and became part of greater Berlin. Marzahn has a particularly dark history. It was the site of a labor camp (today a water treatment plant), where Romas (a group often referred to as Gypsies) were interned two weeks before the 1936 Summer Olympics in Berlin to keep them away from spectators' eyes. As a part of the Nazi extermination policy, up to two thousand Roma inmates remained in the Marzahn labor camp until they were deported to Auschwitz in 1943, where most of them were gassed. In 1941, the *Carl Hasse & Wrede* machine-tool factory was erected in Marzahn and "employed" hundreds of forced laborers. Those who didn't survive the camp or outlive the punishing forced labor were buried at the nearby *Parkfriedhof.* Today, a memorial marks the site. Last on the list of Marzahn's "scars" from World War 2 is its status as the first section of Berlin to be conquered by the Russian army in April of 1945.

Unfashionable Marzahn lies on the far eastern side of Berlin. True to its Communist past, it retains a look that can only be described as bleak. Most of its residents live in the boxy, prefabricated high-rises (*Plattenbauen*) the USSR planted in all of its occupied territories. Although many of these structures have been painted bright colors in a futile attempt to "cozy" them up, the overall landscape in Marzahn feels gray and cold. Unlike other parts of what was East Berlin—such as Prenzlauer Berg, which became hip and trendy when the Wall came down—Marzahn has little to lure tourists architecturally or culturally other than its Gardens of the World.

As Nora described Marzahn's history, Guy wondered what could possibly be worth a trip to Marzahn, which required three trains and two busses from his home in Dahlem. Guy's car was undergoing some much-needed mechanical attention, so he'd been forced to rely on Berlin's excellent mass transit system for several days. Nora assured Guy that he would soon see something truly amazing in this last enclave of the spirit of the former East.

In 1987, Marzahn hosted the *Berliner Gartenschau*, a flower show to commemorate Berlin's 750th anniversary. The show's lavish displays later became permanent features of a "Gardens of the World" project, which most notably included gardens in the Chinese, Balinese, Japanese, Korean, and Italian Renaissance styles. Unfortunately, few visitors to Berlin ever tour the gardens because in 1989, the US State Department issued a warning to American tourists to avoid Marzahn because of its high levels of neo-Nazi activity.

Nora read about the gardens from a brochure given to visitors after they passed through the park's main gate. Guy hid a smile at Nora's obvious pride in being able to read again without his assistance. "What shall we visit first, Guy? The Oriental mosaic courtyard? The labyrinth of evergreen yews? The teahouse on the lake in the Chinese garden?"

"You choose, Nora. We have all day. We can see it all."

"Let's start with the teahouse. I could use a nice hot cup of tea."

Nora felt the need to cram as much as possible into their visit. Although the day was unseasonably warm, it *was* November, and Berlin is famous for a climate that can change dramatically in mere hours. A slight chill was in the air, suggesting that once the sun slipped behind the clouds, the day could become more typical of blustery November in Berlin.

Nora picked a table in the sun on the outside deck of the teahouse. She and Guy shared a pot of fragrant green tea while they plotted their route through the gardens. First, they would stroll through the Japanese complex with its three gardens connected by a network of paths surrounding an inner pavilion. Next was the Balinese complex, "The Garden of the Three Harmonies," which was protected within a glass temple. Then the Korean garden, a gift from the city of Seoul, with its landscape modeled after the geography of Korea. If they had the time before the park closed in late afternoon, they'd end their visit with the Italian Renaissance Garden where the sunny landscape of Italy awaited them.

"Boxed tree topiaries, artfully laid-out paths, stone benches, statuary, a large fountain shell, and numerous potted plants in terra-cotta containers invite visitors on a journey back in time," Nora read from the brochure. "I haven't seen this garden before. It sounds so romantic. Let's make sure we see it!"

"Yes, we certainly must," agreed Guy.

The day stretched luxuriously before them. They wandered from one garden to the next, discussing everything and nothing, just enjoying each other's company. Nora impulsively reached for Guy's hand. "It feels right," she assured herself.

Around five o'clock, long shadows stretched across the Italian garden. Walking slowly through its wrought iron gates, Guy and Nora shared a deep sense of satisfaction. It had been a beautiful day in a beautiful place.

"I have an idea," Nora said. "Let's go to the Adlon and have a drink and decide where we might have dinner. There's a bus outside the park that goes right by the Adlon."

"Good idea. Let's do just that."

Nora was dismayed when she read the schedule posted on the sign at the bus stop. They had just missed their bus, and the next one wasn't due for twenty minutes. "Shall we just walk to the train station? I don't think it's that far. What do you think, Guy?"

Guy was a little reluctant to walk in Marzahn. Apart from the beautiful gardens, the town seemed menacing; but this was Nora's day, so he agreed despite his misgivings. They walked several blocks before the sky darkened ominously. "Nora, it really looks like rain. Let's call a cab."

Nora pulled her cell phone out of her pocket and glanced at the screen. "That's fine with me, but I'm afraid I'm not getting any reception here."

"There's a small tobacco store across the street. It looks a little rough, so perhaps you should let me go in and call for a taxi while you wait here under the street lamp." Guy handed her his ever-present umbrella. "Just in case," he added.

"Thanks," Nora said. After Guy left, she walked a few yards down the street to see if she could get any cell phone reception in another spot. With her head down, eyes fixed on the screen's tiny bars, she failed to notice a group of men approaching her.

"*Guten Tag, Madam,*" said a big burly man who seemed to be the group's leader. He was dressed in black with a T-shirt that read "Fear Me" in Old English script. His neck was encircled by a spiked collar, exactly like the one worn by his big drooling Great Dane. The other men in the group wore similar outfits. Several sported multicolored Mohawks teased to heights of more than six inches.

"*Haben Sie ein Licht?*" Herr "Fearsome" asked, dangling his unlit cigarette in Nora's face. Spotting the silver chain with its Star of David around Nora's neck, his tone changed. "Where do you think you're going, Jew bitch?" he snarled in German.

"Excuse me, sir, but she is not Jewish," Guy said as he approached the group.

"Mind your own business, old man," snarled one of Fearsome's companions.

"She *is* my business. She is my friend." Guy attempted to push one of the T-shirted men aside to pull Nora away from the group. The Great Dane snarled, baring his teeth.

"Primo doesn't seem to like you, old man. Maybe he smells your Jew blood." The dog's owner loosened his grip on the choke chain around the big dog's neck. "Go ahead, Primo, have a smell." With that, the dog was shoved toward Guy. "Get him!"

The Great Dane's massive jaw clamped down on Guy's leg and held on for what seemed like hours to Nora. Moaning softly, Guy collapsed to the sidewalk, his hand clutched to his chest. He lay lifeless at Nora's feet.

"What have you done to him?" she screamed. She whirled around, whipping Guy's umbrella in the air. She drove the tip into the eye of the dog owner who bellowed with pain.

Something ripped the fabric of Nora's heart as she lashed out at the men with Guy's umbrella, striking at them with a vengence she'd never felt before. One of the men who lurked on the fringe of the group shouted, "Let's go, the police are coming!"

The unmistakeable "*wheeooo, wheeooo*" of a Polizei siren filled the air. The group ran, their dog in tow, with a swatch of fabric from Guy's pants still lodged in its huge jaw. Nora sank to her knees. "Wake up, Guy, wake up!" she cried as she cradled Guy's head in her arms.

His eyelids fluttered. "Something in my chest," he whispered. "It feels so tight."

"I think you're having a heart attack. Hold on for just a few more minutes. The police are coming." Nora stroked Guy's forehead. "Just lie still. I'm here. Don't worry."

A green-and-white car with *Berlin Polizei* emblazoned on its side screeched to a stop in front of the American woman holding a distinguished-looking gentleman in her arms. A young officer assessed the situation quickly. "Madam, we need to get him to the hospital immediately. The ambulance is right behind us." With that, a white van pulled up beside the police car; two German

EMTs grabbed a stretcher from the back of the van and gently rolled Guy onto the stretcher.

"May I ride with him to the hospital?" Nora asked in German.

"I will drive you myself," the young officer volunteered.

"Please let him be OK. Please let him be OK," Nora chanted over and over. Her spirits sank when she remembered the last time she'd prayed for a man's recovery. Her prayers went unanswered with Mitch. Would the result be the same with Guy?

Sirens blaring, the police car and the ambulance roared off, bound for the nearest hospital—the *Unfallkrankenhaus Berlin*, in the center of Marzahn. The EMTs skillfully transferred Guy to a hospital gurney which waited for him at the door of the hospital's emergency clinic.

The hours dragged on as Nora sat in the waiting room. She could see doctors and nurses rushing back and forth through the small window in the emergency-room door. Despite her best intentions to stay awake and alert until she heard something about Guy's condition, her head drooped and she dozed off around 10:00 p.m.

"Madam?" A nurse gently shook Nora's shoulder. "You may see your friend now."

"What time is it?" Nora asked groggily.

"It is early morning, around eight o'clock."

"Where is he? Is he OK?"

"He's fine. Come. I'll take you to his room."

Guy was sitting up in bed, drinking a cup of tea and nibbling on a piece of soggy-looking toast. Noting that Nora wore the same outfit as the day before, he asked, "Nora! Were you here all night?"

She rushed to his bedside. "Are you OK? How do you feel?"

"I'm fine. It was a mild heart attack. There was also some evidence that the dog that bit me had rabies, so I've been shot many times."

"I think you want to say that you have *had* many shots," she corrected him. "I thought Primo looked anything but primo," she added wryly.

"Thank you for taking such good care of me, Nora."

"I didn't do anything special, Guy."

"Yes, you did. You defended me. The hospital staff told me that the man you poked with my umbrella has sustained serious injury to his eye. His friends brought him here shortly after I arrived."

"Wouldn't it be something if he has a torn retina?" Despite the seriousness of the situation, Nora couldn't help giggling at the possibility. "It would serve him right."

"The man who works at the tobacco store saw everything. It was he who called the police. He also knew the men who attacked us, and he reported that to the police too. He is a very brave person. I only hope those ruffians don't try to punish him for helping us. And, Nora . . ."

"Yes?"

"He said you fought like a warrior against those men. For that, I am forever in your debt. But I also owe you an apology. If they hadn't seen the Star of David I gave you, most likely, they wouldn't have attacked us."

"You can't be sure of that, Guy. Besides, I believe it was the star that gave me courage—first to tell you about my parents and Mitch, then to fight off those idiots in Marzahn. Who knows what mighty deeds I may still do with the help of my star!"

Guy slapped his leg and laughed appreciatively, then groaned. "I forgot about the ten stitches in my leg."

"Does it hurt much?"

"Only when I laugh, Nora. Only when I laugh."

*　　*　　*

Guy was released from the hospital early the next day. Nora borrowed Cary's car and drove him back to his home in Dahlem. Helena met them at the door. "Please, Herr Guzman, let me help you to your room. I have been worried about you, but I see that you are in good hands." She nodded at Nora. "Frau Reinhart, I heard about what happened and what you did. I owe you an apology. I misjudged you greatly. I thought you were taking advantage of

Herr Guzman's kindness, but I see now that you are a very kind person too—much kinder than I."

"Thank you, Helena, but you don't owe me an apology. You were simply being loyal to your employer. But I do think Guy should rest now. How are you feeling, Guy?"

"With two such good women hovering over me, I feel very well cared for. But I do think a short nap is in order." With that, Guy hobbled to the stairway and made for his room. His leg was clearly bothering him, but his sense of humor remained intact.

*   *   *

Guy recovered quickly. Nora remained at his house long after she had been cleared to fly back to the US. She still hadn't found a way to tell Guy she was leaving. It was Guy himself who brought up the subject. They were sitting in Guy's *Wintergarten*, a sunroom with expansive windows on three sides of the room. Although it was now mid-November, the afternoon was unusually sunny—not at all typical for Berlin in early winter. They sat on an old wicker settee, piled high with pillows, and sipped the strong German coffee to which Nora had become addicted.

"So, my friend, how is your research coming?" asked Guy.

"Fine. I'm pretty much done. I've completed almost two dozen interviews in all—more than enough to write a credible article on my conclusions."

"And what have you concluded?"

"Based on the little bit of research I did, I would say that with some exceptions, Germans who lived in East Germany are much happier with the Wall coming down than Germans who were living in West Germany. Once they got beyond their general euphoria over the idea that the two Germanys are now reunited, almost all the people I interviewed from the West grumbled about the overall cost of reunification. They complained specifically about the amount of money the German government has pumped into updating the trains and the roads and lots of the buildings in what was East Germany. I detected quite a lot of resentment, which seemed to reflect what I've heard described as the 'Wall of the Mind'—which may take another generation or two to disappear. There is more that I could say, but I think that pretty well sums it up."

"I will look forward to reading your article," Guy responded. "And when do your classes begin again in the US?" he added.

"In January—early January," replied Nora, caught off guard. "I really need to get back home and prepare for them," she added softly.

"I assumed you would feel that way. I suspect you extended your stay in Berlin to take care of me. If that is so, I assure you that I'm feeling fine now, completely back to normal. As much as I hate to see you leave, I don't want you to stay just to nurse me."

"Oh, Guy, I've stayed this long for myself as much as for you. I can't tell you how much your friendship has meant to me. I will always treasure the memories of our time together."

"Our time together doesn't need to end, Nora," Guy whispered, reaching for Nora's hand.

She patted the hand that stroked hers. "I know that, but I also know that I've got to do some work on my life before I can consider a life with someone else. You helped me open the doors to a lot of truths about myself, and now I have to go home and deal with those truths. I have to make peace with Mitch, first and foremost."

"How will you do that?"

"I've been thinking about it. In a few months, it will be the anniversary of his death. I want to plan a big memorial for him. It will be my way of saying good-bye to him the right way, the way a loving wife should. I managed to think about everything but Mitch when I was planning his funeral. I want to have lots of time to think about him now, before the memorial."

"That sounds like a wonderful idea."

"I also need to find a way to forgive my parents, particularly my father. I was tested for the BRCA2 gene before I left the US, so I'm in no more danger of getting cancer than any other woman my age. So what my father did—not telling me something so important for so many years—was terrible, but luckily it won't impact my health.

My mom was my mom. She had her flaws. She was *way* too passive when it came to my father, but then, so was I. She was a wonderful mother otherwise. I see her as my only mother. I have no desire to meet my birth mother. Anyway, these are all things I have to sort out, and I'm finally ready to do it, thanks to you."

"No, Nora, it's thanks to *you*. You are the one that is facing these things. I merely, as the English say, 'got the ball rolling down the hill.'"

Nora laughed uproariously. "Yes, you did do something like that!"

"Nora, when you are ready, I'll be here."

"Are you really going to wait until I come back to Berlin to see me again?" Nora's eyes twinkled with mischief. "Christmas is coming, you know, and I have a lovely guest room. After that, there's my spring break. We could do a bit of traveling together then. I could show you all my favorite places in America."

"Like the Grand Canyon? I've dreamed of seeing the Grand Canyon ever since I was a teenager and read Karl May's books about the American West. I was greatly taken with Winnetou, May's wise chief of the Apaches, who appeared in many of his novels."

"Wasn't May a German writer?"

"He was very popular in much of Europe. In fact, he still is. Some years ago, Anais and I traveled to Croatia to visit Plitvice Lakes National Park and stayed at the Winnetou Lodge not far from the park. We laughed and laughed over finding a small corner of Karl May's 'Wild West' in Croatia."

"Then we must see the Grand Canyon. I'll have plenty of time for it after I retire. I've decided that this will be my last year of teaching."

"Are you sure, Nora?"

"Yes, it's time to pursue my dream of living in Berlin. After Mitch's memorial, I intend to come back and find a permanent place of my own in Berlin, so you'd better still be here!"

"You can count on it. I have received an offer to rebuild Berlin's *Stadtschloss*, the city palace. It's to be rebuilt on the site of the former East German parliament, so it looks like I'll be here for a long, long time."

*   *   *

Nora shifted her laptop bag to her other shoulder and turned to wave to Guy, Cary, and Monika. They had all come to Tegel Airport to see her off. She knew that when she passed through the security gates, it could be months before she'd see any of the three again. This saddened her greatly, but at the same time, she was excited about starting a new chapter in her life. She looked forward to a future without guilt, without regrets. She knew it would take lots of painful reflection, delving into memories she had long buried, but she knew she could do it. She'd move through the demanding process of self-examination to arrive at her new future in Berlin. After all, she had lots of good years left in her.

Mitch used to tell her, "Only the good die young, Nora. The feisty ones like you will live forever!"

And that's what she intended to do.

About The Author

J oanna Schultz is a recently retired professor who travels extensively with (and without) her husband. Her favorite destination is--not surprisingly--Berlin. She lives with husband Tom in Ann Arbor, Michigan, where she's at work on a second novel.